"You and I live in different worlds," *Shannon said.*

"Different countries, but that's just geographical. Other than that, I'll bet we have a lot in common."

"I can't imagine what, Michel. You're a ruler, after all. You're used to telling people what to do and having them follow orders. Even if your subjects don't agree with your ruling, there's really nothing they can do about it, is there?"

"Perhaps not, but I don't want to be that kind of monarch. I hope we can put all that behind us. But, why are we wasting time with this now? I want this trip to be memorable for you."

The pinpoints of light in his eyes, as he gazed at her, sent up a warning flag. Shannon was sure that playing Eve to Michel's Adam would be an experience she would never forget, but she didn't indulge in casual flings—not even with a prince.

Dear Reader,

I'm delighted to introduce Barbara Gale, whose intense story *The Ambassador's Vow* (SSE #1500) "explores not only issues involved in interracial romance, but the price one pays for not following one's heart." The author adds, "Together, the characters discover that honesty is more important to the heart than skin color. Recognizing the true worth of the gold ring they both sought is what eventually reunites them." Don't wait to pick this one up!

Sherryl Woods brings us *Sean's Reckoning* (SSE #1495), the next title in her exciting series THE DEVANEYS. Here, a firefighter discovers love and family with a single mom and her son when he rescues them from a fire. Next, a warning: there's another Bravo bachelor on the loose in Christine Rimmer's *Mercury Rising* (SSE #1496), from her miniseries THE SONS OF CAITLIN BRAVO. Perplexed heroine Jane Elliott tries to resist Cade Bravo, but of course her efforts are futile as she falls for the handsome hero. Did we ever doubt it?

In *Montana Lawman* (SSE #1497), part of MONTANA MAVERICKS, Allison Leigh makes the sparks fly between a shy librarian and a smitten deputy sheriff. Crystal Green's miniseries KANE'S CROSSING continues with *The Stranger She Married* (SSE #1498), in which a husband returns after a long absence—but he can't remember his marriage! Watch how this powerful love story unites this starry-eyed couple.... Finally, Tracy Sinclair delivers tantalizing excitement in *An American Princess* (SSE #1499), in which an American beauty receives royal pampering by a suave Prince Charming. How's that for a dream come true?

Each month, we aim to bring you the best in romance. We are enthusiastic to hear your thoughts. You may send comments to my attention at Silhouette Special Edition, 300 East 42nd Street, 6th Floor, New York, New York 10017. In the meantime, happy reading!

Sincerely,
Karen Taylor Richman
Senior Editor

Please address questions and book requests to:
Silhouette Reader Service
U.S.: 3010 Walden Ave., P.O. Box 1325, Buffalo, NY 14269
Canadian: P.O. Box 609, Fort Erie, Ont. L2A 5X3

An American Princess

TRACY SINCLAIR

Silhouette®

SPECIAL EDITION™

Published by Silhouette Books

America's Publisher of Contemporary Romance

SILHOUETTE BOOKS

ISBN 0-373-24499-1

AN AMERICAN PRINCESS

Copyright © 2002 by Tracy Sinclair

TRACY SINCLAIR

began her career as a photojournalist for national magazines and newspapers. Extensive travel all over the world has provided this California resident with countless fascinating experiences, settings and acquaintances to draw on in plotting her romances. After writing over fifty novels for Silhouette, she still has stories she can't wait to tell.

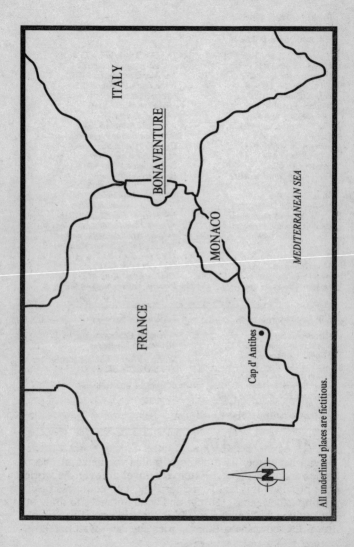

All underlined places are fictitious.

Prologue

The newest and hottest game show on television was *Royal Reward*. Millions of people tuned in every week, and a few hundred lucky ones got to see the show live from the studio in Hollywood where it was broadcast.

The excitement in the audience ran high on this night, the final round that could decide the winner. All eyes were on the stage where two young women stood under twin spotlights. Both contestants were beautiful and brainy, but polls taken during the ten weeks of the contest had picked Shannon Blanchard as the favorite.

Perhaps it was because of her long, shining blond hair, blue eyes and the graceful way she moved. Shannon looked like a princess. Her slender figure was gently curved—sexy, yet elegant—and her soft voice had a quiet assurance.

Gordon Lederer, the emcee, was trying to heighten the tension. "This is the night you've all been waiting for, the night when one of the young women on this stage could receive a Royal Reward. It's been a tough battle. They both outscored the other eight starters to get where they are. Now they have to compete against each other for the grand prize. So, who will it be? Linda or Shannon?"

The audience responded with shouts for their favorite, accompanied by whistles and cheers.

The emcee waited for the tumult to die down before he said, "The answer to my next question could decide the lucky winner. Please be very quiet, audience, because there's a lot at stake here." He turned to the brunette and said, "Are you ready, Linda?"

"As ready as I'll ever be, Gordon," she answered confidently.

"I don't know how to take that," he said to the audience. "Okay, let's get right to it." His jocular manner turned serious. "The legendary English king, Henry VIII, had six wives. To claim your Royal Reward, give me their names and the order in which he married them, starting with number one."

The audience groaned as Linda's confidence vanished and she fumbled for the answer. "Well, uh, there was Anne Boleyn…"

"She was one of them, but not his first wife. I want them in order."

Linda searched her memory frantically, but after a couple of despairing looks at the clock, she only managed to come up with one more name, Anne of Cleves.

"Oh, I'm sorry," Lederer said. "But you haven't

lost yet, Linda. If Shannon can't give the correct answer, you'll both come back next week for another try at the grand prize—two weeks in Europe, living in a castle like a princess!''

As he walked toward her, Shannon was mentally thanking the professor of her world history class in college. Henry VIII had been a particular favorite of hers. The woman had made them memorize every detail of his many marriages.

''How about it, Shannon? This is your big chance to walk away a winner—if you can give me the correct answer.''

The audience went wild when she named all six wives, starting with Catherine of Aragon, and ending with Catherine Parr.

Lederer had to shout to make himself heard over the applause and cheering. ''Congratulations, Shannon Blanchard, you are our new princess! You've won a Royal Reward, two weeks in a castle in Bonaventure, where you'll be the guest of His Royal Highness, Prince Michel de Mornay.''

Shannon felt like pinching herself as he described the glamorous life that awaited her. The castle would be fully staffed, of course, with a butler and a full complement of servants. In addition, she would have a private car and driver at her disposal, plus a lady-in-waiting of her choice. A complete wardrobe would also be provided for all the glittering parties and events she'd attend.

Shannon beamed a big smile and a thumbs-up at her cousin, who was sitting in the first row of the studio audience. Marcie Cole was the one responsible for her being on the show, so of course she would be Shannon's lady-in-waiting.

It was hard to imagine that one correct answer could have such an impact on their lives. Life was certainly funny. You never knew what was going to happen next.

Chapter One

Prince Devon was staring avidly at the only television set in Glenmar Castle, rooting as hard as anybody in the studio audience for Shannon Blanchard.

He leaped from his chair and pumped his fist in the air when she won. "Yes! What a beauty! This should get me out of the doghouse with big brother." He hurriedly turned off the set when footsteps sounded in the hallway.

Television was a touchy subject with his older brother, Prince Michel, ever since Devon had made a deal with the TV game show to host the winner. It was just a practical joke, but Michel didn't see it that way. He was furious. They'd always been close, but this prank had strained their relationship.

"What was all the racket in here?" Michel asked from the doorway of the den. His generous mouth thinned to a straight line as he glanced at the blank screen of the television set. "I presume you were watching that idiotic show again."

"You'll be glad to hear it was the final round. The game is over."

"Why would that make me happy? It means those people will be invading our privacy sometime in the near future."

"Well, actually, quite soon." Devon managed a weak smile. "I guess you could call that the bad news."

"I can't imagine any good news coming from this sorry affair." Michel's gray eyes were stormy. "I don't know how I ever agreed to allow a fake princess to come here. I should have let the studio go ahead and sue us like they threatened."

Devon remained prudently silent. They both knew it was unthinkable for the royal family of Bonaventure to be involved in a frivolous lawsuit. The television show would be delighted, whether they won or lost. It would mean untold free publicity for them. The tabloids would go on a feeding frenzy.

Maybe Michel was right, he conceded ruefully. He did leap into things without considering the consequences.

"They'll be in and out of here before you know it," Devon said placatingly.

"When you say 'they,' how many people are we talking about? There is only one winner, isn't there?"

"Absolutely! A perfectly smashing blonde with an unbelievably gorgeous figure. That was the good news I was about to tell you."

Michel's level gaze wasn't promising. "You

haven't answered my question. How many people are they sending here?''

''You have to understand that this is what they call a prime-time television show. They tend to do things on a rather grand scale.''

''How many?''

''Three or four,'' Devon admitted. ''But you don't even have to know they're here,'' he continued hurriedly. ''I'll have rooms prepared for them in the north wing, and they'll be out and about most of the time. They're not going to hang around the castle all day.''

''When are they coming?''

''They'll arrive on Sunday.'' Devon braced himself for a tirade.

But Michel just uttered an exclamation of disgust and stalked out of the room.

Glenmar Castle was set on a knoll, far from the road below. Glimpsed from a distance, with the late afternoon sun gilding the crenellated towers, it looked like a fairy-tale palace in the sky.

As unreal as everything else that had happened to her, Shannon thought. Less than a week after winning the fabulous vacation, she and Marcie were sitting in the back seat of the sleek black limousine that had met them at the airport. Their eyes were shining with excitement as their heads swiveled from side to side in order not to miss anything.

The two men in the car with them were more blasé. This was just another job to George Hatcher, the public relations man hired by the studio to see that a constant stream of publicity about the show appeared in the media. The photographer, Dave Finley, wasn't even looking out the window. He was busily assembling his camera equipment.

As they proceeded up the long driveway, Marcie exclaimed with pleasure, "Ooh, look at the sheep! Isn't that picturesque?"

She stuck her head out the window to get a better look at a flock of fleecy white sheep grazing on the lawn. Several workmen and a man on horseback were trying to urge them to move on.

"And look, there's even a Prince Charming riding a horse. I wonder if they staged this for our benefit?"

"I doubt it," Shannon said. "He just works here. In fairy tales, the prince always rides a white horse, that one's black."

"He could be a prince. Look at those broad shoulders and muscular forearms. What a hunk!" Marcie said as the limousine slowed to a halt in front of a barrier blocking their way.

"What's that sawhorse doing in the road?" George Hatcher demanded. "Get out and move it," he instructed the chauffeur.

Before the man could comply, the reason for the barrier became evident. Several sheep wandered onto the driveway.

"We can't wait until that whole flock gets across! Honk your horn, that'll clear the road." He stuck his head out the window, waved an arm and yelled loudly, "Shoo! Get out of the way!"

The man on the black horse trotted over and scowled at him. "What the devil do you think you're doing?"

"What part of 'get out of the way' don't you understand?" George countered.

Shannon pulled at his sleeve. "We're guests here," she murmured. "This is no way to start out."

"Let me handle it," he said.

The horseman had turned away and was talking to the chauffeur, ignoring George and not even glancing inside the car at the other occupants. After a few words, he wheeled his horse around.

"Hey! When are you gonna move those sheep?" George called. "We don't intend to wait here all day."

"Then I suggest you look for other accommodations." The man spurred his horse lightly and cantered away.

"Did you ever hear of such insolence?" George fumed. "I intend to report him to the prince!"

"Let it go, man," Dave Finley said. He took the cap off his camera lens and opened the car door. "I might as well get some establishing shots while we're waiting."

George's jaw set. "We better not be here long. What's that man's name?" he asked the chauffeur.

"That's Prince Michel, sir," the man answered.

George was speechless for once, but Shannon exclaimed, "I can't believe it! He's wearing jeans and a cotton shirt like the other men. I thought he was a foreman or something."

"He's 'something' all right," Marcie said. "That rugged face is to die over!"

"He's handsome enough," Shannon conceded. "But he isn't very gracious. After all, we're his guests."

"Paying guests," Marcie reminded her.

"Yeah, that's right!" George said, still stinging from the prince's put-down. "He ought to thank us for being here. Anybody who has to rent out the family castle is obviously strapped for cash."

"Maybe he maxed out his credit cards this month," Marcie said. "But his loss is our gain. Unless he expects us to pitch in with the cooking and cleaning."

"That wouldn't surprise me," George muttered. "He's an arrogant devil."

They all stared at the prince as he deftly rounded up strays. He was a superb horseman. The powerful black stallion responded instantly to his slightest command. Prince Michel ignored them. He seemed to have forgotten they were even there.

The driveway was cleared in a short time, and their car proceeded up to the massive front door of the castle. Their reception this time was warm enough to soothe even George's ruffled feelings.

Prince Devon came out to greet them, while uniformed servants unloaded the luggage. This prince was everything they'd expected—suave, good-looking and regal without being forbidding.

There was a family resemblance between the brothers, but Devon wasn't as strikingly handsome as Michel, nor as tall and athletically built. He was dressed more elegantly, though, and his lighter brown hair was artfully cut.

Michel's thick sable hair had been windblown, Shannon reminded herself. It might look just as well styled when it was combed. But he gave the impression of not caring one way or the other. Her silent evaluation of the two men concluded that Michel might be more exciting—like a roller coaster where you were soaring one minute and bottoming out the next—whereas Devon would be nice safe fun to be with.

The castle exceeded their expectations, from the vaulted grand entry hall, to the branching marble staircase across the vast expanse of gleaming floor.

Devon led them down a broad corridor to a beautifully furnished reception room. Priceless rugs defined different areas of the room, and damask-draped French windows looked out on a formal garden.

"I thought you might like some refreshments after your long trip," he said, when they'd settled into bergere chairs upholstered in maroon satin.

Within minutes, a butler entered the room carrying a heavy tea service. Another servant followed with a three-tiered stand of graduated china plates. Each was filled with small sandwiches.

"If the de Mornay brothers are hurting for money, it sure doesn't show," Marcie murmured to Shannon.

Prince Devon was a charming host. They were all enjoying his anecdotes and their glimpse at the royal way of life. Suddenly a deep male voice called from down the corridor.

"Devon? I want to talk to you!"

The prince moved hurriedly to the door, too late to warn his brother. Shannon and the others could hear a very irritated Prince Michel's complaint.

"You promised me those television people wouldn't get in the way. Shall I tell you the first thing they—"

"Come in, Michel," Devon interrupted hastily. "We have guests."

Michel scowled as he looked over Devon's shoulder and saw George. His expression changed when he glanced around the room and noticed the others.

Devon took advantage of his brother's discomfort. "You haven't met our visiting princess. Allow me to introduce Miss Shannon Blanchard and her lady-in-waiting, Miss Marcie Cole."

When Shannon and Michel's eyes met, the full force of his masculinity hit her. Prince Michel might be imperious and quick-tempered, but he radiated sexuality. No woman could be indifferent to him. Especially when he decided to turn on the charm. Her entire arm tingled when he took her hand and kissed it.

"It's a pleasure, Miss Blanchard."

His husky voice almost made her believe he meant it, but she reminded herself that he was a reluctant host. "I'm sorry if we disrupted your sheepherding this afternoon," she said in a cool voice.

"We didn't know who you were," George said. "I didn't mean to get so testy, but it was a long plane ride. The women were anxious to get here and unpack."

As Shannon gave him an indignant look for blaming his bad manners on them, Devon introduced the other two members of their party.

"We're really thrilled to be here," Marcie said. "This is our first trip to Europe—Shannon's and mine anyway."

"Then it's too bad your show didn't choose a castle in France or Italy." Michel hadn't intended to sound inhospitable, but he realized—too late—that his comment could be taken that way, given his earlier outburst.

Devon explained for him. "Michel meant that cities like Paris and Rome are the places most first-time tourists want to see."

"We weren't given a choice in the selection," Shannon said, flicking a glance at Michel. "So I guess you're stuck with us."

"Or the other way around," Michel drawled, in renewed annoyance. How could such an exquisite woman be so thorny?

"I can't think of any place I'd rather be than right here," Marcie said. "I fell in love with Bonaventure while the plane was still circling for a landing."

The tension in the room suddenly eased. "That's very flattering, but you don't have anything to compare us to." Michel gave her a genuine smile.

"I hope to get to those other places someday, but I'm here now and I intend to enjoy myself."

"What a refreshing attitude, Miss Cole. You're quite a philosopher."

"No, I work in an office at an insurance company. Any change of scenery has to be an improvement." She grinned.

Michel laughed. "Nobody is in danger of getting an inflated ego from you."

Shannon was amazed at how warm and charming he could be—to somebody other than herself. There had been tension between them from the moment they met. Too bad, but they probably wouldn't have to see much of each other anyway.

Dave had taken his camera out of the case. "I'd

like to get some candid shots of everybody. Just keep on talking as if I weren't here.''

"Let Shannon comb her hair first," George said.

"Then they wouldn't be candid shots, man. She looks fine."

They all looked at Shannon. Her long blond hair was windblown, and she had on a minimum of makeup, just a slick of lip gloss and a touch of mascara on her thick lashes. She didn't need anything else. Shannon was that rare gift of nature, a natural beauty.

"She looks better than fine," Devon said. "Wouldn't you agree, Michel?"

His brother didn't answer. Michel was lost in thought, picturing a gentler Shannon with her soft lips parted in anticipation, and her thick lashes lowered provocatively.

"Michel?" Devon raised his voice slightly.

"What?" Michel was suddenly aware that everyone was staring at him. What the devil had he done now? "I'm afraid I was a little distracted for a moment. You were saying?"

"It doesn't matter," Shannon said.

"This tea is delicious," Marcie said quickly. "Could I have another cup?"

"Of course." Devon rang a crystal bell. "I'm sure we're all ready for more. How about you, Michel? Would you like some tea?"

"No, thanks, I have work to do. I hope you have a nice stay." He included all of them in the general pleasantry.

After Michel had left the room, Dave said, "I wish

I'd gotten off a few more shots. It doesn't look like we'll be seeing the prince again very soon.''

''He'll be at the reception tonight, won't he?'' Marcie asked. Devon had told them he'd planned a small gathering for that night, so they could meet some of the local gentry.

''I'm hoping Michel can join us, but he might be tied up with some obligatory state affair. My brother takes his duties as ruler of the country very seriously.''

''I've been meaning to ask you about that,'' George said. ''Isn't the head of state usually called king instead of prince?''

''In most instances, yes,'' Devon said. ''But there are exceptions—like Monaco, for instance. It's a matter of long-standing tradition.''

Shannon didn't take part in the conversation. She was puzzling over Michel's attitude. He couldn't even pay her a meaningless compliment, prompted by his brother. Why had he taken an instant dislike to her?

A short time later, Devon said, ''It's been such a pleasure getting acquainted that I'm afraid I've kept you here much too long. You must want to get settled in your quarters.'' He rang the bell again. ''I'll have you escorted to your rooms.''

When they reached the top of the marble staircase, a servant led Marcie and the two men down one corridor, while another man led Shannon in the opposite direction. She didn't say anything until they had walked the length of the hall and made a right turn. They seemed to be in a different wing entirely.

"I thought my room would be near my friends," she said tentatively. "Are you sure this is right?"

"Prince Devon told me to give you the princess suite," the man said. "Would you like to speak to him about changing your accommodations?"

"No, I'm sure whatever he chose will be lovely." She was already in Michel's bad graces, she didn't want to alienate Devon, as well.

When he opened a pair of carved double doors and ushered her inside, Shannon's eyes widened. The living room of the suite was exquisitely furnished with Oriental rugs, down-filled chairs covered in silk and satin and a delicate antique writing desk. The walls were hung with paintings in carved gold frames, and a large Venetian mirror was centered over a curved, tufted sofa.

A breeze coming from slightly ajar double French doors on the far wall made the prisms tinkle on a crystal chandelier. After the servant left, Shannon wandered over to look out at the view. She discovered the doors opened onto a terrace that ran the length of that wing of the castle.

"Shannon? Are you in there?" Marcie's voice came from the hall outside the suite. "Holy cow, I've never seen anything like this, even in the movies!" she exclaimed after Shannon had opened the door.

"That's just make-believe. They don't know how a real princess lives," Shannon said in an affected voice, twirling around in front of the mirror.

"Neither do you. Don't start believing your own publicity or you'll be in for a big letdown when we go home."

"We just got here!"

"I know. Isn't it wonderful?" Marcie flopped down on the sofa. "Two full weeks of royal living. What could be more perfect?"

She glanced around the room consideringly. "You know, I'm changing my mind about the de Mornay brothers being broke. Maybe Devon talked his brother into letting us come, and now Michel is having second thoughts."

"I can't imagine anyone talking Michel into anything. He is, without a doubt, the most autocratic man I've ever met! No wonder he's still a bachelor. What woman would want to be his princess?"

"You've got to be kidding! Can you imagine what it would be like to make love with the guy?"

They were both silent for a moment, each picturing her own erotic scene. Shannon's involved the prince's nude body twined around hers in jasmine-scented darkness, his husky voice murmuring sensuous words in her ear as he caressed her body intimately.

She took a breath and exclaimed, "We sound like a couple of high-school girls fantasizing over a movie star. Let's go look at the bedroom. I haven't seen it yet, myself."

"What have you been doing?"

"Just drinking in all this luxury. There's a terrace outside those French doors with a gorgeous view of the grounds."

"I have to see it!"

Their voices carried as they enthused over the formal flower beds and rolling green lawns. Adding a romantic touch were two white swans swimming gracefully across a pond in the distance.

Devon stuck his head out of a room at the other

end of the terrace. His curious expression changed as he exclaimed, "What are you two doing here?"

"Shannon was showing me the view," Marcie said. "I must say I'm impressed—by everything."

"You were doing a little exploring on your own?" He glanced over his shoulder for an instant. "I intended to give you the full tour tomorrow. It's getting late, though. I imagine you want to get ready for the reception. Why don't I walk you back to your rooms?"

"Shannon is already here, but I'd be delighted to have an escort," Marcie said.

"I can't thank you enough for my beautiful suite," Shannon told him. "I'm sure you were the one responsible."

"Oh, well…" Devon said. "I'm glad you like it. If you'll excuse me, I have to speak to someone." He returned along the length of the terrace with long strides.

Marcie frowned thoughtfully. "Devon seems upset. Do you think we did something wrong?"

"Not yet, but I'm sure his highness the prince will find something to complain about."

"Don't be so hard on the guy," Marcie said as a knock sounded at the door.

Even George was impressed by Shannon's elegant accommodations. After inspecting the room thoroughly, he said, "At the reception tonight, I want you to tell everybody how thrilled you are to be staying in a castle, and how exciting it is to meet a real, live monarch. You know, give it the wide-eyed Cinderella treatment."

"That's so phony," Shannon protested. "I *am*

happy to be here. Why can't I just say so and let it go at that?''

"Work with me, baby. With my publicity machine and your looks, you could have a career in show business—if you play along, that is.''

"I don't want to be in show business. I have a stimulating job of my own.''

"Everybody wants to be in show business,'' he stated. "But okay, then do it for the producers. You owe them big-time. They've spent big bucks on you. Your wardrobe alone cost thousands.''

"While you two fight it out, I'm going to take a bubble bath,'' Marcie said.

Devon had hoped to avoid his brother until he straightened out the unfortunate mix-up. But Michel entered the room before he reached the door to the hallway.

"Michel! I didn't expect to see you.''

"This is my apartment.''

"Well, yes, of course. I meant, I thought you were in your office going over reports, or something. You're a regular workaholic. Not that that's a bad thing,'' he added hastily.

Michel sighed. "If something is wrong, Devon, why not tell me and get it over with?'' As his brother started to profess ignorance, he said, "I can always tell when you're trying to slide something by me.''

Curiosity overcame Devon's concern. "You saw through me even when we were boys. How do you always know?''

A smile transformed Michel's handsome face. "If I told you, you'd have to develop a new technique, and I'd have to waste time figuring it out. So, tell me what's bothering you."

"I'm afraid there's been a slight...um...mix-up."

"What kind of mix-up?"

"I instructed Jennings to prepare a suite for Shannon fit for a princess. He evidently misunderstood, because he gave her the Princess Suite—the one next to yours." Devon's words tumbled over each other in his haste to explain. "I know I promised they wouldn't get in your hair, but this honestly wasn't my fault. I'll fix it though, don't worry. If it's any consolation to you, I really painted myself into a corner this time. Shannon has been raving about her quarters. I don't know what reason I can give for moving her out, but you know me. I'll dream up some plausible excuse."

Michel's forbidding expression had vanished. "Is that what you're so upset about?" He grinned suddenly. "It isn't as though you put her in my spare bedroom. Leave her where she is. She won't bother me."

"I'm afraid she'll be out on the balcony at all hours. That's how I discovered Jennings's mistake. Shannon and Marcie were outside, rhapsodizing over the grounds."

"Is Marcie sharing the suite?"

"No, she's in the north wing with the others. But she'll probably be popping in and out of Shannon's room."

"Well, if they get too noisy, I'll ask them to turn down the volume."

"You're being awfully decent about this, Michel. From now on I promise you won't be bothered—and this time I mean it!'' Devon looked at his watch. ''I'd better get ready for the reception tonight.''

''What time are the guests coming?''

''Around eight. I'm having it in the large drawing room, so you might want to avoid that wing. When people ask for you, I'll tell them you had to attend a state dinner.''

''Don't do that. It would sound inhospitable of me. After all, they *are* guests here. I can drop by for a short time.'' When Devon looked uncertain, Michel laughed. ''Don't worry, I'll be pleasant—even if it kills me.''

After his brother left, Michel went into his bedroom, a large, very masculine room that reflected his personality.

He was whistling as he turned on the shower in his marble bathroom. Tonight might not be so bad after all, Michel decided. Shannon was probably as sorry as he that they'd gotten off on the wrong foot. The next two weeks could turn out to be quite memorable.

Chapter Two

The reception was like something out of an old-time Hollywood movie. A string quartet in a corner of the large drawing room provided soft background music as elegantly dressed men and women chatted and sipped champagne. Servants glided unobtrusively among the guests, refilling glasses and offering silver trays filled with hors d'oeuvres.

"Do you get the feeling that Cary Grant is going to come sauntering in at any minute now? This is his kind of party," Marcie said. "I could definitely get used to living this way," she murmured as Devon approached with a distinguished-looking man.

Shannon had wondered what she would find to talk to these people about, but the conversation flowed easily. Not like her attempt at small talk with Michel. Would it do any good if she made a special effort to

be more agreeable? Not that she expected—or desired—any kind of romantic relationship with him.
But if they could manage to be pleasant to each other,
it would ease the strained atmosphere and make her
stay more comfortable.

She didn't expect him to show up at the party, but
when Michel did appear, she felt a rush of pleasure.

It didn't mean anything. Most women would react
the same way, she told herself. He looked very suave
in a superbly tailored dark suit and a snowy-white
shirt that accentuated his deep tan. Shannon couldn't
decide if he was more attractive this way, or in jeans
with the sleeves rolled up and his hair all windblown.
Their eyes met and Michel smiled.

George picked that moment to take Shannon's arm
and draw her aside. "You're not promoting the show
enough. When anybody asks how you like being a
princess, play it up big," he said in a low voice. "Tell
them how thrilled you are to be staying in a real,
honest-to-God castle. These social things get written
up in the newspapers."

"We'll talk about it later, George." She was very
aware of Michel approaching their little group.

"What's to talk about? I'm just asking you to display a little enthusiasm," George said. "People back
home want to hear about your dream vacation."

"So far, this isn't a vacation. Nobody told me I
was going to be a walking advertisement for a television game show."

"There's no free lunch, kid. This trip is costing the
production company plenty. Can you blame them for
wanting to get their money's worth?"

A flash of anger made her eyes sparkle like sapphires. She and George were due for a long talk, but now wasn't the time. "Okay, I'll try to say all the right things," she said, to end the discussion.

He seemed satisfied, because, to her relief, he moved away.

The prince and Marcie were chatting together easily. Shannon was trying to think of something to say so she could join in, when Michel turned and included her in the conversation. "Marcie told me that you two are cousins."

"Yes, first cousins. Our mothers were sisters." Brilliant repartee! Shannon thought disgustedly. Why was there this constant tension between them that always made her either say the wrong thing, or else sound stupid? She was actually grateful when George returned, bringing some people with him.

"The Countess Lewellan wants to talk to you, Shannon," he said. "She thinks the local newspaper might be interested in doing a feature story on you."

"It's such a lovely Cinderella tale," the older woman said. "Everybody will want to read about you."

"Especially since the prince is your own handsome Michel," George said. "Right, Shannon?"

"Please, George, you're embarrassing me," she said through gritted teeth.

"It's all right, my dear." The countess laughed. "All the young ladies are in love with Michel."

"Now *I'm* the one who is embarrassed." Michel didn't look any happier than Shannon.

"What do you think of our little country?" the countess asked Shannon.

"It's simply charming. We just arrived today, but

I'm looking forward to seeing a lot more of Bonaventure. I love all the greenery, and of course this castle is magnificent.'' There, that ought to satisfy George, she thought. It was even the truth.

''The castle is centuries old, but Michel has modernized the plumbing and heating system, and so on. I know those things are important to Americans,'' the countess said.

''In a gorgeous setting like this, I'd be willing to overlook a few amenities.''

Shannon expected her flattering words would please Michel. Instead, he was frowning. What did it take to satisfy the man? she wondered in exasperation.

From across the room, Devon noticed Michel's displeasure and hurried over to smooth whatever discord had arisen. He'd been pleasantly surprised that his brother had chosen to attend the reception. What could have gone wrong so soon?

''Is everyone getting acquainted?'' Devon asked in a hearty voice when he joined their group.

''The countess has been most gracious,'' George answered for all of them. ''She's going to set up an interview for Shannon with the local media, and I'll try to see that the wire services pick it up. Bonaventure will get a lot of publicity out of this, I promise you.''

As Devon suppressed a groan, Michel said, ''If you'll excuse me, I see someone I must speak to.''

Shannon watched as he threaded his way across the room. Michel did stop to talk to a few people, but only for a couple of moments. Then he went out the door.

The prince was fuming as he went up to his apartment. He had been willing to give Shannon the benefit of a doubt, but his original impression of her had been correct. She was as shallow and self-serving as he'd supposed.

Her gushing tribute to Bonaventure and the castle was merely a ploy to get publicity, and the countess had fallen neatly into her trap. Shannon had certainly manipulated the poor woman deftly.

What did she hope to gain? Perhaps she intended to write a book about her experiences here. It seemed that everyone who had ever been in the same room with a so-called celebrity, wrote a book about it.

More probably, though, Shannon was angling for a career in show business. She was lovely enough, no question about that. Her soft lips and camellia-petal skin could inspire poetry. Too bad her beauty was only skin-deep.

Shannon was up early the next morning, even though she'd gotten to bed quite late. She'd always been an early riser. Besides, there was too much to see and do here to waste time in bed.

After dressing in jeans and a U.C.L.A. T-shirt, Shannon applied a touch of lip gloss, tied her long hair with a pink ribbon and pinned it to her crown. Everyone seemed to be asleep, but her sneakers didn't make any noise as she walked down the grand staircase and out the massive front door.

It was a picture-perfect April day. The colorful flowers surrounding the castle softened the ancient stone walls, and the blue and gold pennants flying from the crenellated turrets fluttered in the soft breeze.

Shannon crossed the circular driveway and walked down a gravel path, enjoying the birdsong and the brightly hued butterflies that fluttered like graceful dancers.

The brilliant sunshine became muted when she followed the path into the woods. The castle disappeared, leaving her in an enchanted green world. She lost track of time as she strolled along the mossy path, stopping to admire clumps of wildflowers or to listen to rustlings in the underbrush.

After a while, a bench by the side of the trail was a welcome sight. Shannon sank down onto it gratefully and tilted her head back. She'd been walking for at least an hour. The sound of horse's hooves in the distance snapped her out of her reverie. As she gazed down the path, a splendid black horse came thundering toward her.

Michel almost didn't recognize Shannon in jeans. His first reaction was annoyance that he'd have to stop and make stilted conversation. Courtesy demanded it.

But when he reined in his horse and got a better look at her, he had to admit she was a pleasure to behold. The filtered sunlight turned her hair different shades of light and tawny gold that were a stunning contrast to those amazing blue eyes.

"You're up early," he said as he slid off the horse.

"I've always been a morning person."

"Even when you've been partying until late the night before?"

"Yes."

Michel could have kicked himself when her voice

turned cool. Why had he alluded to the reception after the tension there'd been between them last night?

In an effort to lighten the atmosphere, he said, "Do you have big plans for today?"

"Not for today, but I can't wait to see more of Bonaventure. It's so old-worldly and gracious. If George has other plans for me, that's unfortunate. I intend to do a lot of sightseeing."

"Can you do that without his approval? He seems to be calling the shots."

"Not after we have a long talk." Her chin set grimly. "I had no idea that my visit here was going to be used to publicize the show."

Michel hesitated, not wanting his skepticism to show. Then they'd be back at sword's points again. He tried to make his tone nonjudgmental. "Didn't you wonder why they sent an entourage with you?"

"They didn't tell me that George and Dave were coming until we were ready to leave. I certainly had no idea they were sent along to plan my agenda. George even puts words in my mouth. The things he makes me say don't sound like me at all."

"Does that mean you don't think Bonaventure is beautiful, and I'm not Prince Charming?" Michel asked in amusement.

She returned his smile. "That's one of those trick questions where whatever I answer is wrong."

"Not necessarily. Everybody likes to receive compliments."

"I'm sure you receive a lot of them."

"People wanting favors or a government position don't count. A compliment from a beautiful woman is always welcome," he said.

"So, can I take that to mean you've forgiven me for disrupting your household?" His surprising friendliness this morning encouraged Shannon to get everything out in the open. "None of us realized that your brother had made the deal for us to come here without consulting you."

Michel's cheekbones sharpened. "That was his idea of a practical joke. He was shocked to find out the television people weren't any more amused than I was when he attempted to break the contract. I've tried to make him see that he has to be more responsible—after all, he's second in line for the throne!"

Shannon could sympathize, but she understood Devon's viewpoint, too. He was a fun-loving young man with unlimited resources and no responsibilities. The chance of his ever becoming ruler of Bonaventure was slim to nonexistent. Michel was young and virile. He would marry and have sons who would succeed him, sometime far in the future. She didn't say any of this, naturally.

"Just about the only thing Devon and I argue over is his irresponsibility," Michel continued. "We've always had a close relationship, especially since our parents died."

"That was terribly sad," Shannon murmured.

She remembered being told that their mother and father had contracted a deadly virus while paying a state visit to a small emerging nation. Michel had ascended the throne three years ago when he was barely thirty. The country had been in shock, but he'd proved to be a competent and charismatic leader.

Michel suddenly seemed to realize that he was discussing personal matters with a virtual stranger.

"Anyway, I just wanted to explain my rude behavior."

"You had every reason to be upset, but I think I can offer you a ray of hope for the future. It wouldn't surprise me if George and Dave went home soon. After I tell him today that I won't take part in his publicity campaign, I can't see why either of them would stick around."

"Won't that be damaging to your career?"

"I'm a paralegal. I work for a very dignified law firm that has nothing to do with television or the movie industry."

"Isn't that why you went on the program? To break into show business?"

Shannon shook her head. "I never wanted to be on the show in the first place. It was all Marcie's idea. She suggested we send in our names—along with hundreds of other women. You have no idea how they hyped the show ahead of time. I told her I wasn't interested, and when she couldn't change my mind, she filled out an application for each of us without telling me. I should have suspected something when she asked me for a snapshot of myself. Why would she need it? We see each other several times a week! It didn't occur to me at the time, though."

"You had to send in a picture with your application?"

Michel could understand how Shannon had been selected. She was as beautiful this morning as she'd been last night in a glamorous outfit and full makeup. Her hair was like sunshine in the light that filtered through the trees, and her tight T-shirt was as alluring to him as her sequined sweater had been the evening before.

She was aware of his admiring yet circumspect glance. Perversely, it didn't please her. "I know what you're thinking, but the show wasn't a beauty contest for airheads. The questions were easy at first, I'll grant you, but when serious money became involved, they got quite difficult."

"I thought the prize was a two-week European vacation and the title of princess. I didn't realize any money was involved."

"There wasn't, if you took a chance and went for the grand prize. The winner got the trip and all that went with it. But until the last round the contestants won money for answering questions correctly. If they missed a question they were eliminated from the game and lost everything, but they could drop out before the final round and keep what they'd already won. I wanted to quit halfway through and take the money, but the producers and Marcie talked me out of it." Shannon grinned suddenly. "She's darn lucky I won. I'd never have let her hear the end of it if I hadn't."

"Why would you want to quit?"

"I could have used the money to pay bills, and I didn't really want to be a princess."

"Was that before or after you met me?" Michel teased.

"It was nothing personal." She returned his smile. "I'm just a very private person. I didn't like all the notoriety I got from being a contestant on a national game show. You kind of become public property. People recognized me wherever I went. I couldn't dress like this because they expected me to be glamorous even if I just went to the grocery store for a quart of milk.''

"I'm sure you wouldn't disappoint anyone looking like you do today.''

"You're being kind. The worst part, though, was that people felt free to ask the most amazingly personal details of my life. I can just imagine what it must be like if you're royalty!''

"It's slightly different. They don't ask direct questions. They just speculate on whether the sensational gossip written about you is true, false or a little of both,'' Michel said sardonically.

"At least you have a few perks that make it worthwhile.''

"That's true. I get invited to a lot of parties, and all the pretty girls have to dance with me.''

"I'm sure they would anyway,'' Shannon remarked lightly. "There must be other rewards. You don't strike me as the frivolous type.''

"No, that's Devon's department. The second in line always has more freedom.''

"He's just high-spirited. I doubt if he's purposely trying to aggravate you.''

"I suppose you're right. Some of the stories about past royals make Devon look like a choirboy. The de Mornay family has had its share of borderline delinquents. When I lose patience with my brother's antics, he reminds me of Prince Norbert, the third son of the currently reigning monarch. Norbert once put an ad in the newspaper, saying furnishings from the castle and selected pieces of the crown jewels would be sold on the front lawn.''

"I wish I'd been at *that* estate sale!"

"You wouldn't believe the crowd of people that showed up."

"Yes, I would. What happened when they found out it was a hoax?"

"They were allowed onto the grounds and placated with refreshments. I can just imagine how the kitchen workers had to scramble. But that was only an inconvenience. The concerned messages from foreign countries worried about their investments in Bonaventure were a real headache. They thought the country had gone bankrupt."

"Devon will never top that caper." Shannon laughed.

"I often think he's trying."

"What happened to Prince Norbert? Did he get locked in the tower and put on bread and water?"

"I don't know, but if he was, it wouldn't surprise me if he played three-card monte with the jailer and won the key to his cell."

"I wish I had colorful ancestors like that. The only eccentric in our family was Aunt Kate. She did wheelies on her bicycle until she was almost eighty. But that doesn't put her in Norbert's class."

"It's pretty impressive, though." Michel smiled.

Since he could see that Shannon was truly interested, he told other stories about his ancestors. The glimpses into his impressive dynasty told her where he had gotten his mixture of charisma and high-handedness.

"I'm being a very bad host," he said finally. "I've done all the talking."

"I enjoyed listening to you. It's fascinating to hear about real princes and princesses."

"You see, we're people just like you."

"Well, I wouldn't say that. You and I live in different worlds."

"Different countries, but that's just geographical. Other than that, I'll bet we have a lot in common."

"I can't imagine what. You're a ruler, after all. You're used to telling people what to do and having them follow orders."

"I wish!" Michel said. "I have to enact laws that aren't always popular. So then I have to explain that I'm acting in the best interests of the country."

"Even if your subjects don't agree with your ruling, there's really nothing they can do about it, is there?"

"Perhaps not, but I don't want to be that kind of monarch."

Shannon gave him an admiring look. "I can't believe I misjudged you so badly. You're really something else!"

"I'm not familiar with the expression, but it sounds positive."

"It is. I'm sorry we got off to such a bad start—"

"Which was my fault," he interposed quickly.

"Not entirely. But anyway, I hope we can put all that behind us and be friends."

"I'd be honored," he said, gazing into her eyes.

Shannon was acutely aware of everything about him, the faint scent of a woodsy aftershave, his thickly lashed gray eyes that seemed to read her thoughts. She hoped not! It would be so embarrassing

if he knew she was thinking that he was the hand-
somest man she'd ever met.

"If we're going to be friends, I'll need to know
more about you," he said, putting her at ease. "So
far, I only know that you won a television contest,
and Marcie is your first cousin—on your mother's
side," he teased, reminding her of last night's reception when that was all she had found to say to him.

It was a mark of how far they'd come in such a
short time that they could joke about it, Shannon reflected. "You must have thought I was a real lame-
brain!"

"On the contrary, I thought you were adorable—
frustrating, but definitely alluring. My brother did,
too. You've captivated the entire royal house of de
Mornay."

"There are only two of you."

He raised a dark, peaked eyebrow. "How many
princes does it take to satisfy you?"

Michel could do it all by himself. He must be very
experienced in the art of making love. She could
imagine their bodies molded together while his firm
mouth softened against hers and his hands caressed
her sensuously.

Shannon's pulse quickened at the erotic vision and
she said hurriedly, "I was merely remarking that you
have a very small family—although it's larger than
mine. I was an only child, and my father died when
I was a teenager."

"That's sad. There are only you and your mother
left?"

"Not even that. She's gone now, too. Mother became ill when I was in my last year in college."

"U.C.L.A.?" He looked at the letters written across her chest.

"Yes, it's a state school. Not as expensive as a private university, but not cheap, either. I managed to get my degree, but I couldn't go on to law school. I needed to get a job and take care of mother. Then after she died I had enormous bills to pay, so graduate school wasn't an option. I'd planned to specialize in family law, because I've always had a great rapport with children."

"I'm afraid I don't see the connection."

"Family law covers divorce and custody cases, among other things. I'd like to be an advocate for the poor kids who often turn out to be the real victims. Too many parents use their children as bargaining chips for their personal gain, or to cause their spouses grief."

He nodded. "Yes, I've seen that happen. It can be very ugly."

"It's reprehensible! If you could see some of the cases that come through the office it would break your heart."

Michel seemed disinterested when she cited case histories involving troubled children—which wasn't surprising. He was a glamorous bachelor with more immediate things on his mind. His focus would change when he got married and had his own family.

He did seem interested in her career choice. "You said you were a paralegal. Isn't that a lawyer?"

"No, we work for attorneys, and take care of a lot of legal matters, but we don't have a law degree. We can't argue cases in court. That takes more years of college, which so far, I haven't been able to afford."

"That's too bad." He really looked sympathetic.

"I can't complain. I have an interesting job and I like the people I work with. Someday, when I get out of debt, I still plan on going back to school for my degree. I would have been a lot closer to my goal if I hadn't let Marcie and the others talk me out of quitting and taking the money I'd won."

"It would have been sensible, but I'm glad you didn't," Michel said warmly. "I promise to make this trip so memorable that you won't have any regrets."

The pinpoints of light in his eyes, as he gazed at her, sent up a warning flag. They were all alone in a leafy paradise with only the birds and the butterflies as witnesses. Shannon was sure that playing Eve to Michel's Adam would be an experience she would never forget, but she didn't indulge in casual flings—not even with a prince.

Glancing at her watch, she exclaimed, "It can't be this late! George must be having a minor seizure. We're supposed to do a photo shoot at ten o'clock."

"I thought you were going to declare your independence."

"I am, but I don't want to be unfair to anybody. The producers did spend a lot of money on me. I figured I'd do this one last photo shoot—let Dave take as many pictures as he wants of the castle and me—if that's all right with you?" She looked at Michel questioningly.

He shrugged. "He'll take them anyway, one way or another. I've had experience with the paparazzi."

"I'm sorry," she murmured.

"Don't be. Just give me one of the photos. I'll hang it with my collection. Of other royalty who have visited here,'' he added with amusement at the disapproving look on her face.

Shannon felt properly foolish for thinking he was referring to a gallery of pinup girls. She attempted to hide her discomfort under a light tone. ''That's quite an honor, but if I don't get back to the castle there won't be any pictures. I'm going to be terribly late as it is. I walked for an hour before I got to this spot. Do you know of a shortcut through the woods?''

''I have a better suggestion. Why don't I give you a lift?''

''On your horse?''

''It's better than walking.''

''Okay, I don't mind if the horse doesn't.''

''Zeus will be honored.''

He lifted her in his arms and set her astride the powerful black stallion that had trotted over in answer to his whistle. Then Michel put a foot in the stirrup and swung into the saddle behind her.

Shannon eyed the horse warily. It seemed a long way to the ground from up there. ''He's very big, isn't he?''

''Don't worry, I won't let you fall.''

''I notice you didn't say he's gentle,'' she remarked wryly.

''No, but he respects authority.''

''I hope Zeus remembers that he's the horse and you're the master.''

''We settled that a long time ago.''

When Michel put his arm around her waist and settled her body spoon fashion against his, Shannon stopped worrying about the horse. It was obvious that

Michel could handle him. He had the hard chest and muscular limbs of a champion athlete.

He inspired confidence, but when the horse broke into a rhythmic canter, Shannon gripped Michel's arms.

He tightened the arm around her waist and said, "Just relax. We'll be home in a few minutes."

How could she relax when his warm breath tickled her ear and his masculinity enveloped her like a sensuous cloak. She turned her head to look up at him, but that was a mistake. Their lips were only inches apart.

Somehow she found the strength—and good sense—to face forward again. Neither of them acknowledged the moment, but both were affected by it. They didn't speak until Michel reined up at the front door of the castle.

He dismounted and held up his arms for her, saying, "There, wasn't that better than walking?"

"It was quite an experience." She gripped his broad shoulders as he put his hands on her waist and swung her to the ground.

"You're trembling!" he exclaimed, drawing her into his arms and smoothing her windblown hair. "I had no idea you were this frightened. Why didn't you tell me? I would have slowed down."

Shannon allowed herself just a moment to savor the heady intimacy of his embrace. Then she drew away. "I wasn't really frightened, just a little… apprehensive. Zeus is rather daunting, and I haven't been on a horse since I was ten. Anyway, thanks for getting me back on time. I'd better go up and change." She hurried toward the front door.

Michel watched until she had disappeared inside. His eyes were narrowed in thought as he walked over and vaulted into the saddle. When his brother appeared a few moments later, Michel raised a hand in greeting but didn't stop to talk.

Devon stared after him with a worried expression. "I hope nothing *else* happened," he muttered under his breath.

Chapter Three

Shannon didn't have time to dwell on what she chose to call "the small incident" with Michel. She had barely gotten into her room when there was a knock at the door.

"Shannon, are you in there?" George's muffled voice sounded annoyed. "I've been calling you on the house phone for an hour!" When she opened the door he stared at her in outrage. "Look at you! I told you we were going to take publicity pictures this morning. Why aren't you ready?"

"I will be in a few minutes."

"Your hair is a mess, you don't have on makeup. What have you been doing all morning?"

"I went for a walk."

"All this time? Where did you walk—to Paris?"

She bit back the things she wanted to say. That

would come later. "Wait for me downstairs, George. I won't be long."

"You need to do more than slap on a little lipstick. I'm going to try to get one of the popular magazines to do a spread on you, with the castle as a backdrop. Then after we finish here we'll shoot at some scenic spots around town. Maybe I can plant a story in that upscale travel mag—what's its name? Well, anyway, bring plenty of outfits to change into. This will take all afternoon."

Shannon's patience ran out abruptly. "You'd better get all the pictures you need at this shoot, because I'm not posing for any more after today."

"What are you talking about? Dave and I are here to document your entire trip. In fact, I've been giving some thought to ways we can hype the story. It would really fly off the stands if we can get some cozy shots of you and Prince Michel—you know, hint that there's something romantic going on between you two."

"How can you even suggest such a thing?" she exclaimed.

"I'm not asking you to go to bed with the guy— although a lot of women wouldn't consider that a hardship. He's got quite a reputation with the ladies."

"I'm not interested in hearing about it," she said curtly.

George wasn't listening. "His brother, Devon, does, too. Maybe there's an angle there. We could play on the love triangle bit. Hint that the two brothers are fighting over you."

"George!" Shannon said, loud enough to get his attention. "You're not going to plant any phony stories about the royal family or anything else. Because if you do, I'll tell the reporters the truth, that it was all a stunt to get publicity for the show.''

"You can't do that! Where's your gratitude?''

"For what? Promising me a glamorous trip and then ruining it for me?''

He called her ungrateful and reminded her again of how much the producers had done for her. When that didn't do any good, his expression turned ugly and he resorted to threats. She had agreed—at least tacitly—to cooperate. The show might have grounds for making her repay what they'd spent on her.

Shannon let him get it all out of his system. When he finally ran down, she said, "Threats can work both ways. What kind of publicity do you think the show would get if I told the newspapers what you wanted to make me do for a prize I'd already won? The tabloids would love the part about faking a romance with Michel and Devon.''

First George blustered, then he wheedled, finally he pleaded.

Again Shannon waited him out. When he couldn't think of any further inducements, she said, "You'd better not waste any more of your last day. I'll meet you downstairs.''

Shannon had changed into a blue summery dress with a full skirt and cap sleeves. With it she carried a large-brimmed straw hat with a circlet of roses and long blue satin streamers, an outfit suitable for a garden party on an estate. At least that's what she hoped, never having been to such an affair. Her reception from the people assembled on the front lawn was positive.

"I love that outfit!" Marcie exclaimed.

"You look like a princess," Devon agreed.

"That color is gonna be a knockout against the green grass and the gray stone walls," Dave said. "Let's start over there by the path. That way I can get the castle in the background."

Shannon posed on the lawn, by the massive carved front doors, by the pond dabbling her fingers in the water as the two photogenic swans swam toward her.

She posed with her hat off, and with it on, although she warned that it would muss her hair. Not that she minded; she was trying to cooperate with Dave.

"That's okay, it looks sexy a little mussed up," he said. "Now take it off again and pretend you're going to throw it like a frisbee. That's it. Perfect!" he said as she laughed, showing even, white teeth.

When Dave had shot photos of Shannon in every pose and location on the front acreage, he sent her to change clothes. "Wear something casual this time, as if you're going for a stroll in those woods down there. Maybe white pants and heels—the higher the better. And try to make it snappy. I don't want to lose the light."

Shannon could have told him that nobody hiked in high heels, but she didn't argue the point. "Is there somewhere down here where I can change clothes, Devon? I brought a lot of outfits downstairs so I wouldn't have to waste time going all the way back to my room. They're on a chair in the entry right now."

"Of course, let me take you someplace where you can have privacy."

Picking up her clothes from the chair as they entered the castle, he led her to a room that was smaller than the luxurious den or the grandly proportioned reception rooms. This room must be his office. A large desk facing the door was piled with papers and official-looking documents. There were also a couple of metal file cabinets. So, Devon wasn't really an inveterate playboy. That was just the image he cultivated.

"I'm afraid it's a little messy in here," he remarked as he draped over a couch the garments he'd helped her carry.

"It's fine. Thanks for your help."

After he'd left, Shannon removed her dress and the pale blue bra she'd worn underneath. It would show through the white silk blouse she planned to wear with linen pants and a brightly colored scarf knotted around her waist. She was looking for the outfit among the pile of clothes on the couch, when the door opened.

She straightened up, startled. Her breath caught in her throat as she stared disbelievingly at Michel.

He was equally startled, but his expression changed as he gazed at Shannon's exquisite body. For a moment he thought she was completely nude. Then he realized she was wearing sheer-to-the-waist panty hose.

The smoldering look on his face alerted her, and she grabbed a dress and held it in front of her body. "How could you just walk in on me like this? You're supposed to be a gentleman!"

"I'm sorry. I didn't know…"

"You could have knocked!"

"Well, yes, but I…"

"What are you doing here anyway?" she demanded.

Could he possibly have thought she *wanted* him to find her like this? Did he think she'd been sending him signals during that intimate ride on Zeus? Shannon was furious at his presumption!

"This is my office."

"What? I just assumed it was Devon's. I asked him where I could change clothes. Why would he bring me in here?"

"I was taking Zeus back to the stable. Devon must have thought I was going for a ride, instead of returning from one. I'm usually gone for at least an hour, so he didn't think I'd be using my office."

"That must have been it," she murmured. "I should have known you wouldn't do something like this on purpose."

"I'm the one who's sorry for barging in on you."

"Yes, well…I'd like to get dressed." She was burningly aware of being almost naked under her flimsy shield.

"Of course! I'll leave you alone."

Shannon hastily scrambled into her shirt and pants, trying to blot out the image of his avid gaze traveling over her bare breasts. Don't overreact, she told herself. Nude women were no big deal to Michel.

She ran a hasty comb through her long hair and checked her makeup in a mirror on one wall. Her cheeks were blooming like scarlet roses, but she didn't have time to put cold water on them. Hopefully the others would think she had on too much blusher.

Michel was waiting for her outside in the hall. As she stiffened warily, he said, "I hope this unfortunate incident won't ruin our budding friendship."

"No, of course not." But she looked somewhere over his shoulder instead of straight at him.

He took her chin in his palm and turned her face to his. "You have a beautiful body, Shannon. I enjoyed looking at you, as I would have enjoyed one of the exquisite paintings in a museum. Can't we let it go at that?"

"It might take me a little while," she said with a crooked smile.

"Not too long I hope."

His velvet voice teased her nerve endings and she backed away. "I'm not as sophisticated as the women you're accustomed to. I'll admit I'm embarrassed right now, but I'll get over it."

Devon rounded the corner and stopped abruptly on seeing them. "Oh! I didn't expect you back so soon." He looked at his brother with consternation. "I... uh...I let Shannon use your office to change clothes."

"Yes, we figured that out," Michel said with amusement.

"Is everything all right?" Devon asked a bit nervously. "Dave sent me to find out what's keeping you."

"I'm on my way out there now," she said.

Both men accompanied her, one on each side.

When they got outside, George said, "Hey, there's

a photo op if I ever saw one! Don't the three of them look regal? Quick, get off a few shots, Dave.''

''I thought we discussed this.'' Shannon's mouth thinned in annoyance.

''It's all right, I don't mind,'' Michel said.

''We always have our picture taken with visiting princesses.'' Devon smiled.

''Good, then it's all settled. Where do you want them, Dave? Let's go!'' George was anxious for the photographer to get started before any of them changed their minds.

''The gazebo might be a nice setting,'' Michel suggested.

''Where is it?'' Dave asked. ''I didn't see one.''

''Come, I'll show you.''

They walked past a rounded tower wall to a secluded area where a lacy white gazebo with morning glories twined around the latticework provided dappled shade a short distance away.

''Oh, Michel, it's charming!'' Shannon said.

Dave nodded. ''Yeah, this will work.''

For the next few minutes he told them where to stand and how to act, clicking his shutter rapidly while he gave directions.

''Don't look at the camera. Pretend I'm not here. That's good. Laugh it up more, Shannon. Now lean against the railing and tilt your head back.''

''That's great!'' George said. ''Maybe you could get them standing closer together.''

Dave didn't even bother to answer. He just continued to concentrate on his job.

Finally Devon said, ''Why don't we get some pictures with Marcie?''

She was standing on the sidelines watching. "Shannon is the star of this show. Nobody's interested in me," she said.

"I'm interested," Devon said. "And I like to think I'm somebody."

"He's right," Shannon said. "Marcie should be in the pictures. I should have thought of that myself."

"It's okay. I don't feel left out, honestly," Marcie assured her.

"She doesn't want to, so leave her alone. We've gotten enough here, Dave," George said hastily before Marcie could change her mind. "Let's find another spot."

"Are we going to give up that easily?" Michel asked the others. "I'm sure we can persuade Marcie to change her mind."

"We'll keep on coaxing you," Devon told her.

George wasn't stupid. He knew when he was outnumbered. Trying to hide his irritation, he said with forced playfulness, "Come on, Marcie, get in the picture. I guess you didn't know how popular you were."

"No, *you* didn't know." Her eyes sparkled mischievously.

When George was finally satisfied that they had enough exterior shots of the castle grounds, he asked Michel to suggest some points of interest in the town or its surroundings where they could take more photographs.

"Change to something less casual," he instructed Shannon. "And bring another broad-brimmed hat. That one with the roses was very flattering."

Michel frowned. "You've been working her too hard. She needs to take a break."

"It's all right," Shannon said. "I promised George I'd give him the entire day. After that, my time will be my own."

"Well, we have to talk about that," George said. "I spoke to Phil Kuzloff this morning." He was one of the producers of the TV show. "He's very disappointed in you."

"That's unfortunate. I'll go change clothes. Have the car brought around so we don't waste any time."

"Wait a minute! We have to discuss this."

Michel had been listening disapprovingly. "I hope you're not going to let him bully you into anything," he said to Shannon.

"Don't worry, I'm not as gullible as I used to be. I've learned to say no and mean it."

"You're a late bloomer. Most beautiful women learn that in the cradle." Michel's eyes lit with laughter.

"Do you want me to come with you into town?" Marcie asked Shannon.

"Not unless you want to. Why should you waste *your* day?"

"Perhaps you'd like to see something of Bonaventure instead," Devon suggested.

"I'd love to! As long as Shannon doesn't mind."

It was a long afternoon. Shannon assumed the different poses Dave requested and smiled for the camera until her jaws ached. Around town they drove to several different locales that looked fascinating—the courtyards of ancient churches, quaint shops that would have been fun to poke around in, so many places she'd have to save for another day.

By the time they finally returned to the castle at twilight, Shannon was hungry and just this side of cranky. She had missed breakfast, and lunch consisted of a quick sandwich eaten in the car. George had resigned himself to making the most of the time she'd allotted him.

It didn't help Shannon's disposition that Marcie was bubbling with enthusiasm over *her* day. She and the two princes were having a drink in the den while they waited for her to return.

"Oh, Shannon, you should have been with us today! Devon took me to the most fabulous places."

"I'm not surprised. I only caught glimpses as we drove around, but everything looked very interesting." Shannon tried to sound upbeat because she really was happy for her cousin.

"You missed the grand tour, but if you have the evening free I could show you our nightlife," Michel said. "Would you care to go out to dinner and visit some clubs afterward? Perhaps Devon and Marcie will join us. He knows more about that scene than I do."

"Don't pretend you lead a monastic existence," Devon said teasingly. "You've been glimpsed out and about fairly frequently.

"Yes, well, the ladies aren't interested in hearing about our lives in depth."

"Can you go to a restaurant like regular people?" Marcie asked.

Michel smiled. "We're a somewhat democratic

monarchy. I have the same privileges as the rest of my people.''

''You know what I mean.''

''People don't prostrate themselves, or cheer and throw flowers when he passes by,'' Devon teased.

''That might be nice—the flower shower, not the prostrate bit,'' Michel joked. ''I must run that past the next session of the royal council.''

''You're making fun of me,'' Marcie pouted.

''Never!'' Devon lifted her hand to his lips.

''You can't blame us for having a lot of misconceptions,'' Shannon said. ''You're the first royals we've ever met.''

''Then we'll have to be on our best behavior,'' Michel said. ''Will you have dinner with me tonight?''

''I'd love to!''

''That's one of your better ideas, brother. Marcie?'' Devon looked at her questioningly.

''Count me in, if you three don't mind going out with a commoner,'' she said.

''We're prepared to be tolerant if you are,'' Devon answered.

The restaurant Michel chose looked like a miniature chateau from the outside. It had stone walls covered with ivy, and even a pennant flying from an angled flagpole over the double front doors.

On the inside, white linen covered tables were spaced throughout the large dining room under crystal chandeliers that cast a soft, flattering glow. Each table was set with china dinner plates and an array of crystal glasses—tall goblets for water, tulip-shaped ones for white wine and bubble glasses for red wine.

They were met at the door by an obsequious maître d'. "It is an honor to have you dine with us this evening, your highness. May I seat you in a private room?"

Michel looked questioningly at Shannon. "Would you prefer a private room, or would you rather have a table here in the main dining room?"

"Whatever you decide will be fine," she said.

"Marcie, do you have a preference?"

"Well, as long as you asked, I'd like to sit out here where everybody can see who I'm with." She grinned.

Shannon groaned. "I can't take her anywhere."

Michel merely laughed.

The dining room was filled with beautifully dressed men and women who were aware of the two princes but too well-bred to stare. Several people, who were evidently acquaintances, did greet the men as they passed, but in a restrained manner. Shannon and Marcie were the ones who got discreetly curious stares.

"There, you see," Michel said, after they were seated at a choice table by a window overlooking a lily pond. "We're treated like anyone else."

Shannon doubted that everybody got this royal treatment. Their table was surrounded by a phalanx of men anticipating their every need. A busboy filled their glasses with ice water, another supplied bread and butter. A waiter brought large menus in leather folders as big as photo albums. Then the tuxedo-clad sommelier, who looked like an ambassador except for the silver cup on a chain around his neck, came to confer with Michel about his wine preference.

When the wait staff had left them alone for a moment, Michel said to Shannon, "I'm glad to see you finally doing something *you* want to do."

"Me, too. You'd have been proud of me. George pulled out all the stops, but after a while I just tuned out. Poor guy, I can't help feeling sorry for him, though. The studio execs must be putting a lot of pressure on him."

"You're not going to weaken and let him spoil your vacation?"

"I don't feel *that* sorry," Shannon said, and laughed.

"Now that your time is your own, we'll have to make some plans," Devon said. "I presume the first thing on your agenda is sight-seeing. May I offer my services? I'm an excellent tour guide."

"I can vouch for that," Marcie said.

"You'd better check your calendar before you make any dates," Michel told his brother. "You have some official commitments coming up, like the reception tomorrow afternoon for the visiting ambassador."

"I thought the Lord Chamberlain was supposed to play host to the ambassador," Devon protested. "They're old friends."

"He will attend, of course, but you'll be the host."

"Why?"

"Because protocol demands that a member of the royal family preside, and you're second in line for the throne."

"That's like being second in line to buy tickets to

a sold-out rock concert. My chances of getting in are nil. Not that I even want the job. You're much better at it than I could ever be.''

''This is neither the time nor the place to discuss it.'' Michel's autocratic expression precluded further argument. His face softened as he turned to Shannon. ''Don't worry, I'll see that you don't miss anything while you're here.''

After looking at his brother thoughtfully, Devon didn't renew his protests.

The slightly awkward moment was glossed over when the waiter came to take their orders. Other than that one slight incident, the evening was a pure delight.

They were finishing dinner when Marcie said, ''Hey, something just occurred to me. How are we going to get around tomorrow? If George and Dave go home, do we still get to use the car?''

''We should be able to,'' Shannon said. ''That was part of the prize.''

''Not to worry,'' Devon said. ''We have plenty of cars you can choose from.''

''That's generous of you, but we need the chauffeur. We wouldn't know where to go, or how to get anywhere.''

''Neither Shannon nor I have any sense of direction,'' Marcie said. ''We're entirely capable of wandering across a border and creating an international incident.''

''We wouldn't want that to happen,'' Michel said. ''Devon will be busy tomorrow, but I can rearrange my schedule. I'll take you.''

Surprisingly, Devon didn't renew his grumbling.

Instead, he said to Marcie, "Would you like to come with me to the reception? I don't know how stimulating you'll find it, but there will be plenty of food and champagne."

"It sounds like my kind of party," she said.

"You've obviously never been to one of these things. We should plan a real party for them, Michel, maybe a dinner dance."

"It sounds fine to me, but that's your department."

"I'll help," Marcie said. "I give great parties. Everybody says so, don't they, Shannon?"

"Yes, but I don't think these guests will want to play charades or pour their own drinks," Shannon teased.

"Then I suppose the clam dip is out, too, huh?"

"It sounds very innovative," Devon said tactfully. "But we can iron out all the details later."

After they had finished their coffee, Michel suggested they go someplace to dance. When they got up to leave, the waiter still hadn't brought a check. Shannon supposed the restaurant just sent a bill to the castle. After all, Michel wasn't going to skip town. Wasn't it ironic, though? The more money you had, the less you had to carry around.

The club they went to had muted lighting and soft music. A dance floor in the middle of the room was filled with couples swaying to the gentle rhythm.

When they were seated at a table, Shannon said, "This is nice. The clubs at home all seem to be so noisy."

"We have those, too," Michel said. "We'll go to one the next time, if you like. I just thought you might prefer this, after the hectic day you've had."

Shannon was constantly amazed at how thoughtful he was. Michel could be imperious, as she supposed he had to be on occasion. But he seemed to be a really warm, caring person underneath.

When they had given their order for after-dinner drinks, Michel asked Shannon to dance.

He was an excellent dancer, as she would have expected. Her body responded to his slightest direction, although he held her in a loose embrace. The dim lighting and romantic music were soothing, generating a seductive warmth that slowly enveloped her.

Desire blossomed deep inside her, like a bud unfolding its petals in time-lapse photography. She was aware of the strength and virility of his lean frame, his muscular thighs, the masculine scent of his skin.

What a wonderful lover he must be, Shannon thought dreamily. Michel could introduce her to a world of sensation she'd never experienced before. He would know how to arouse her almost unbearably—and then to satisfy her completely.

"Are you having a good time?" Michel was smiling at the rapt look on her face, not realizing he was the cause of it.

His low, husky voice brought her to her senses. Yes, he was a genuine Prince Charming, but she wasn't a real princess. Maybe it didn't make a difference in fairy tales, but it did in real life.

Michel could never get serious over someone like herself, even though she could tell he was attracted to her. The potent chemistry between them had been evident from their first meeting, but that wasn't enough for her. She couldn't make love casually— even though she knew it would be an experience she'd never forget. Or maybe that was the reason.

Chapter Four

After the two couples returned to the castle that night, Marcie came to Shannon's suite to discuss the evening. They both agreed that it had been fabulous. The dinner was wonderful, the club afterward was elegant, but most of all, both Michel and Devon were delightful company.

"It was the best date I've ever had," Marcie said rapturously.

"You couldn't call tonight a date," Shannon objected.

"They escorted us to a restaurant and took us dancing afterward. They paid for everything and they brought us home. I call that a date—the kind I could get used to."

"But it isn't as if they had a choice. I mean, we were wished on them. They wouldn't have *chosen* to take us out—at least Michel wouldn't have."

"How can you say that after the way he arranged to be alone with you tomorrow? Poor Devon got stuck with that state function just so Michel could spend the day with you without us tagging along."

"He would have asked you to come, too, if Devon hadn't invited you first."

"You don't really believe that, do you? Michel would have found some way to get rid of me."

"That's not true. He likes you."

"I know, and I like him, too. He just likes you better, or should I say, differently?" Marcie grinned. "My feelings aren't hurt. I say, go for it. If life drops a prince in your lap, enjoy him."

"The man takes us out to dinner *one* night, and right away you read all kinds of ulterior motives into the invitation. Michel was just being a good host."

"Yeah, sure! How do you explain the sparks that fly between you two? Are you going to deny that you're attracted to him?"

"Any woman with a pulse would be. Michel is handsome, he's charismatic, he's intelligent. I could go on and on, but what's the use? He's also the ruler of Bonaventure."

"So?"

"So, I'm a paralegal from Los Angeles. A lot more than an ocean separates us."

"I wasn't suggesting you marry the man. That would be nice, but fairly unrealistic. People do have romances, though. This isn't the Victorian age, and Michel isn't the sort of guy you're apt to meet again in this lifetime."

Shannon was sure of that, especially after this evening. Her body still glowed at the memory of being cradled against his. She didn't have to speculate any longer. Michel could arouse passions that had been sleeping until now, waiting for him to awaken them.

She shook her head slightly and murmured, ''I want my first time to mean more than great sex.''

''What did you say?'' Marcie exclaimed.

Shannon had been lost in her own world, experiencing temptations she knew she'd regret giving in to. She'd forgotten her cousin was even there.

''You can't mean you're still a virgin?'' Marcie was staring at her incredulously.

''I know it's considered unnatural nowadays. People would either laugh or think there is something wrong with me. Like you do.''

''No! I was just surprised, that's all. It *is* a little unusual at our age. Why didn't you ever tell me?''

''It's not something you talk about. What was I supposed to say? Where do you want to have lunch— and oh, by the way, I'm a virgin.'' Shannon smiled wryly. ''It's kind of hard to work into the conversation.''

''I noticed that you never joined in when the rest of us were dishing about guys,'' Marcie mused. ''We all knew you had plenty of men who were crazy about you, so we thought you were just…reserved.''

''*Prudish* is the word you're avoiding,'' Shannon said dryly. ''Go ahead and say it.''

Marcie stared at her consideringly instead. ''Haven't you ever been tempted? You've gone with some great-looking guys.''

Shannon sighed. ''What can I tell you? I guess I've been waiting for bells to ring and stars to streak across the sky.''

"Michel could do that for *me*."

"I want a relationship, not a fling. When I do meet the right man, he'll want the same kind of commitment I do."

"I hear what you're saying, but it's too bad. You could have had a memorable vacation."

"It can be just as memorable, without all those games men and women play. I intend to enjoy every minute of my visit here, especially my time with Michel. And when it's over we'll be friends, and I won't have any regrets."

"I admire your strength of character," Marcie said. She got up from the couch and yawned. "Well, I'll let you get to bed. We both have a big day tomorrow."

While she was getting undressed, Shannon thought about their conversation. She knew Marcie was sure she was concealing some traumatic event that was responsible for her decision not to have casual sex. The truth wasn't that dramatic, although her brief fling with Charlie had upset her at the time.

She had met him right after she realized that graduate school wasn't an option. It was a low point in her life, and Charlie was a welcome antidote. He was an attentive listener, and he made her laugh.

He was also older and very experienced. He had set out to seduce her and he had almost succeeded, even though Shannon realized that she wasn't in love with him. But that didn't seem to be a prerequisite among her friends. Charlie's sensuous caresses were arousing, and she had to admit she was curious to see what she was missing. After holding him off for weeks, she was ready to take the big step.

It was a rude awakening to discover, quite by accident, that Charlie was married, a little detail he'd neglected to mention. She confronted him with the fact, expecting him to fumble around for excuses, but he wasn't even embarrassed. He said she was making a big fuss over nothing. He and his wife had an open marriage. They were both free to have affairs, so what was the harm?

When Shannon lost her temper and told him he was on the bottom rung of the evolutionary ladder, Charlie told her to get real. It was a recognized fact that monogamy was unnatural. Men and women were going to sleep around, that's the way it was. He said she needed to grow up; sex was no big deal. In fact, it would do her good.

The experience, distasteful as it was, turned out to be a good thing. It caused her to reassess her values. She didn't love Charlie, so why on earth had she considered sleeping with him? It was at that point that she decided to use her own judgment and not be pressured into doing something that wasn't right for her, just because other people were doing it.

Michel was the first man she'd met who could set off those Roman candles she was waiting for. She was not only physically attracted to him, she liked and admired him enormously.

Part of her wanted to stop being so cautious, to experience the sensuous pleasure he could bring, even though it would be a brief encounter. But common sense told her to be wary of Michel. This wasn't just another Charlie. Michel could break her heart.

Michel called Shannon on the house phone the next morning. "You said you get up early, so I took a chance that I wouldn't wake you," he said.

"You didn't. I just got out of the shower."

"You can take your time getting dressed. I'm afraid I'm going to be slightly detained."

She was delighted that he wasn't canceling, but she felt obligated to let him off the hook. "Do you want to give me a rain check? I'll understand."

"No, certainly not. I'm looking forward to today. I'll only be about half an hour late, but I didn't want you to rush for no reason."

"That was very thoughtful of you. Actually I'm glad you called. I was wondering if I should wear a skirt or pants."

"Whichever you like, but wear comfortable shoes. We'll be doing a bit of walking, if that's all right."

"It's the only way to see anything. I never could understand taking one of those bus trips where the tour guide tells you about various attractions and then drives by so fast that you only get a glimpse."

"You don't have to worry about that today. I'll see you at ten-thirty instead of ten o'clock."

Shannon used the extra half hour to try on and discard several outfits. Her dressing room looked like a boutique by the time she settled on lemon-colored pants and a yellow silk shirt knotted at her slim waist. Her white fisherman's sandals were rubber soled and comfortable, as Michel suggested.

She was still ready before ten-thirty, so she went downstairs, intending to stroll around the gardens. A limo was pulled up outside the front door, where George and Dave were watching their luggage being stowed in the trunk.

"You're leaving, right now?" Shannon exclaimed in surprise.

"Isn't that what you wanted?" George was obviously not in a mood to forgive her.

"No, I just wanted to be let off the leash. I didn't expect you to leave so abruptly. I thought you'd want to see something of Bonaventure as long as you're here."

"The studio execs weren't interested in paying for a vacation," Dave said. "They told us to get home on the double."

"I'm really sorry."

"Don't be. I have plenty of assignments waiting for me, and George is still on the payroll," Dave said.

"Well, I'm glad they didn't hold you responsible," she said to George. "I'll be glad to tell them it wasn't your fault."

"You can do better than that," he said. "If anything develops between you and Prince Michel, I want to be the first to know."

"Nothing is going to develop," she said firmly.

"You never can tell. He's a handsome guy, you're a beautiful gal. There could be a Hollywood ending."

Shannon rolled her eyes at Dave. "Make sure he gets home all right. George is out of touch with reality."

"I'm just saying *if* something happens. It doesn't have to be Michel. If he's out of your league, how about Devon?" George looked thoughtful. "He's a prince, too. Not the chief honcho, but in some ways he'd make better copy than his brother."

"Forget it," she said. "Devon and Marcie are becoming good friends."

"Really? She's full of surprises." George thought

it over for a moment. "It doesn't have the same PR value, but it *would* be a royal wedding."

"Who said anything about a wedding?" Shannon exclaimed. "I said they were friends."

"George cuts right to the chase." Dave grinned. He took the lens cap off his ever-present camera and said to Shannon, "How about a couple of final pix before we go?"

Michel came through the front door as Dave was snapping rapid shots of Shannon. Frowning, he asked her, "Have you changed your mind about today?"

"No way! I'll be with you in a minute. George and Dave are leaving for the airport."

"It was nice meeting you, your highness." George extended his hand. "I'm sorry about that little misunderstanding we had when we first arrived."

"It's forgotten," Michel said graciously. "I hope we made you comfortable here." He included Dave.

After a short exchange of pleasantries, they all said goodbye.

As he got into the limo, George called, "Don't forget, Shannon. If I'm right, I want to know about it."

The car drove off, to her great relief.

"What was that all about?" Michel asked.

"Oh, you know George," she answered vaguely. "Are you ready? I can't wait to get started."

Shannon had assumed they'd be driven in a limousine. To her surprise, a man in a mechanic's coverall brought a low, silver-gray sports car to the front door.

When Michel noticed the look on her face, he said, "Would you rather take a different car? Fred brought the Lamborghini because it's the one I usually drive, but you can have your choice. Devon is a car buff, so we have quite a collection.''

''No, this one is very sporty. I just expected something black and stately.''

''You're describing a hearse,'' he teased as he helped her into the low-slung car.

''You know what I mean. You're the ruler of a country. At home, even mid-level government officials use limos with a driver, and sometimes a secret service agent, when they go anywhere.''

''Such loss of privacy is a lot to expect of a public servant,'' Michel remarked as he turned out of the castle grounds onto the highway.

''You'd be surprised at how many candidates there are for those jobs, at least partly for perks like that.''

''I suppose it's all in how you look at it. It's strange,'' he mused. ''We're a monarchy, but in some ways we have more freedom than you do in your country.''

''You certainly have a different way of life. I'm still getting over the shock of being alone with you, without an entourage following us around.''

''That would defeat the purpose. I went to a lot of trouble to get you all to myself today.''

So Marcie was right! Unless he was joking. ''Should I take that as a warning?'' Shannon asked lightly.

''Or you could consider it a promise.'' He turned his head to give her a mischievous smile.

She thought it wise not to react. ''Aren't you supposed to be describing the scenery?''

"At the moment there isn't much to see except pastures. This is horse breeding country."

"It looks like a landscape painting," she commented.

The undulating, emerald-green acreage and bright blue sky dotted with a few fluffy white clouds looked like an artist's composition. A couple of sleek brown horses were grazing in the foreground as though posed there, and a white-fenced riding ring was set back from the road.

The traffic picked up when they approached the city, and the urban scene was fascinating in a different way. Michel pointed out various landmarks—an ancient church that dated back to the fourteenth century, a modern office high-rise set between much older, more individualistic buildings.

"Some people welcomed that office building as a sign of progress," Michel remarked. "Others saw it as urban blight."

"I think that's the same all over the world. People don't like change." Shannon grinned suddenly. "Actually that works in your favor. You'll have your job for life."

An unreadable expression sobered Michel's face for a moment. Then he smiled. "It also helps to be born to the right parents."

He pointed out a stately building behind a high grilled fence, and started to tell her its history. Shannon nodded at the right intervals, but she was only half listening. What nerve had she hit with her joke about his having lifetime tenure? Every monarch did. Then she remembered his parents' untimely deaths. Was Michel reminded of the uncertainty of fate—or did he secretly chafe at having had to assume responsibility at such a young age?

She stole a look at him. He was heartbreakingly handsome with his dark hair ruffled by the breeze, and his eyes crinkled against the bright sunlight. His partially unbuttoned silk shirt displayed a deep tan that made him look very virile. If Michel regretted not being as free as his brother, he was doing a good job of concealing it. The whole idea was probably sheer fantasy on her part, Shannon decided.

A newer addition to the city was more acceptable to his subjects, he told her. Sandwiched in among the commercial businesses were a number of small pocket parks with benches and fountains. The park near the middle of town was centered by an ancient-looking cannon.

When Shannon commented on the fact, Michel said, "It's a relic from the distant past. Nobody knew what to do with it, so they stuck it in that park."

"It must have great historic value. Should those children be climbing all over it?"

"Which are you concerned about, the cannon or the children?" he asked wryly.

"Nobody wants a child to get hurt. But the cannon is kind of neat, too. You can't go to the nearest hardware store and buy another one."

"We don't even need that one. Bonaventure hasn't had a war in over a hundred years."

"That's a pretty impressive record. How did you manage permanent peace?"

"When you're a country as small as Bonaventure, you learn to get along with your neighbors."

They had lunch at a weathered tavern that was once

a wayside inn for travelers in the days before automobiles, Michel told Shannon. There was still a hitching post outside.

The interior had been modernized with the essentials like electricity and running water, but the fixtures were crafted to look like oil lamps, and there were candles in wall sconces.

From their table by a window they could look out over a pretty little stream. A pair of ducks were gliding effortlessly over the smooth surface. As they watched, the mother duck climbed out of the water, followed by her brood. A line of tiny ducklings waddled after her, squawking their disapproval.

"Oh, look, Michel, aren't they adorable?" Shannon exclaimed. "They're telling their mother they don't want to come out of the water. Babies are all alike, no matter what the species—strong willed," she laughed.

"You're certainly fascinated by babies."

"Most people are." That wasn't true in his case, she realized belatedly. "I mean, they're so sweet and cuddly."

"I suppose so. I've never known any personally, except Devon, and that was a long time ago. All I can remember is that I expected a playmate, but he slept most of the time."

"Your mother must have been pleased, even if you weren't."

"I suppose so." He picked up his menu. "May I suggest some of the specialties here?"

They lingered so long over lunch that there wasn't time for Michel to show her all the things he'd planned.

"We'll have to pick up next time where we left off," he said. "Maybe it's just as well. You would probably enjoy the flea market, and they only hold it on Fridays."

"I love flea markets, but can you take another day off?" Shannon asked, just to hear him say he enjoyed her company. She certainly enjoyed his!

"The country runs just as well without me, but I'd prefer that didn't get around," Michel chuckled.

When they returned to the castle, the butler told them that Devon and Marcie were waiting for them in the library.

"We were just about to send out a search party," Marcie exclaimed. "You've been gone all day!"

"It didn't seem like it," Shannon said. "I hated to see the day end."

"She's trying to make points with her host," Michel said, but he looked pleased.

"Where did you go?" Marcie asked. "Did he take you to the Royal Museum? The guidebook says not to miss it."

"We didn't have time today, but it's definitely on my list. I hear they have a wonderful collection of old masters."

"Forget the Rembrandts. You can see those any-where. The crown jewels are kept in the museum."

Shannon gave the men a wry smile. "Marcie makes jewelry. That's why your art collection takes second place to the crown jewels. Her things are really beautiful. The pendant she had on last night was one of her pieces."

"I noticed it," Michel said. "It was lovely."

"It's just a hobby," Marcie murmured, looking embarrassed. For once, she didn't have a smart comeback.

"You're very innovative," Devon said. "Maybe you can get some ideas from our jewel collection. We'll have to make a date to check it out."

"Is tomorrow too soon?" she asked.

He laughed at her eagerness. "I'm afraid so. Michel and I will be tied up for the next couple of days. The annual awards ceremony is tomorrow, here at the castle. That will last all day. Then on Thursday, we have to go to a family wedding in Cap d'Antibes."

Shannon knew it was unrealistic to expect two royal princes to spend all their time with them. She shouldn't be disappointed, but she was. Their stay here was so limited.

"You and Shannon are invited to the awards ceremony tomorrow," Michel said. "If you'd care to come, that is. Don't feel obligated. I must warn you that it entails a lot of pomp and ceremony."

"We'd love to come!" Shannon said, without needing to check with her cousin. "It sounds interesting. What are the awards given for?"

"It's a way of expressing appreciation. Various people are recognized for meritorious service and rewarded with titles or medals."

"Maybe I can get some design ideas from the medals," Marcie remarked.

"It's possible, but we'll still go to the museum," Devon said. "I'll call the curator and arrange for a private showing on Friday. That should give him time to assemble all the pieces. Only a small selection is on public display.''

"Friday would be great," she said. "Or any other day, if that's inconvenient. We'll still be here for over a week and a half."

"That's not so long."

"Not long enough. But I'm lucky to be here at all. If Shannon had missed that last question, we'd both be sticking TV dinners in the microwave right now."

"We'll try to do better than that," Michel said. "Have you heard or read about any place you'd like to try for dinner tonight?" He included both women in his query.

"We had such a big lunch," Shannon said. "I don't really want very much."

"I'm not hungry either," Marcie said. "You should have seen the food they had at the reception."

"Shall we have dinner here, then?" Michel asked.

After they had all decided that was a good idea, Shannon said, "I want to hear about the reception."

"It was a hoot!" Marcie told her. "There were all these distinguished-looking gentlemen with red satin ribbons across their chests, and shoulders full of medals. It looked like a Viennese operetta. I expected somebody to break into song at any minute."

"You were lucky," Michel told her with amusement. "It sounds like this was one of our livelier receptions."

"Surprisingly, it was," Devon said. "Marcie could get a totem pole to respond. You know how hard it is to talk to Ambassador Charmaneau? He agrees with everything you say, but he never volunteers anything on his own. Well, you won't believe it, but Marcie had him chattering like a squirrel. I don't know how she does it.''

''It's not hard,'' she said. ''You just ask about their families, or their hobbies, something personal. People like to talk about themselves. The ambassador was telling me about his grandson. The kid's a real brat and the parents don't know what to do with him.''

Devon gave her a shocked look. ''I can't believe he told you something that personal!''

''Why not? He was upset, and he needed somebody to talk to. He couldn't very well discuss it with you.''

''Or Michel,'' Shannon said. ''Bachelors are bored by children.''

''Actually, Michel is very good with them,'' Devon said. ''Several of our friends chose him to be godfather to their children.''

Shannon had observed Michel's lack of interest firsthand. His main function as a godparent must be to send beautiful gifts on appropriate occasions. She didn't voice her opinion, however.

Soon afterward, they all went upstairs to dress for dinner.

Michel had ordered dinner to be served in a smaller dining room than the formal one, which could seat thirty-six comfortably.

Their table was set as beautifully for the four of them as for a state dinner. Tall tapers cast a soft glow over the antique flatware, the centerpiece of fragrant white roses and the array of wineglasses at each place setting. The multitude of servants that glided in and out of the room unobtrusively anticipated their needs without being asked.

While they were eating, Devon mentioned the dinner dance he'd planned. "I thought we'd have it on Sunday. Is your calendar clear for that night, Michel?"

"I'll see that it is," his brother answered.

"Can you get together a big party on such short notice?" Marcie asked.

"It's one of the perks we have," Devon answered. "People rarely turn down our invitations."

"So you don't know if they want to come, or if they have to," she teased.

"You learn to live with that." Michel's smile didn't seem quite as spontaneous.

Shannon realized for the first time that even a life of unbelievable luxury and privilege came with a price. Did that account for the way he often seemed unapproachable? Or the fact that he'd never been seriously involved with a woman, at least not long-term.

But that was nonsense, she told herself. Who wouldn't want Michel, with or without his money and power? Her breathing quickened as she gazed at his handsome, laughing face. There was a man who didn't seem to have a care in the world.

It was a lovely, relaxed evening. After dinner they had coffee on the side terrace overlooking a garden. The flowers were shadowy in the darkness, but their perfume scented the soft breeze.

Shannon refused Michel's offer of an after-dinner drink. "It would put me right to sleep. It's been a full day."

"We'll make it an early evening. Tomorrow is going to be another busy one."

"I'm looking forward to it."

"I'm glad you're coming. I want you to see that I do attend to royal business now and then," Michel joked.

"I'm afraid we haven't given you much time for it lately."

"I can't think of anything I'd rather have been doing," he said with a melting smile.

"Isn't this where you're supposed to agree with your brother?" Marcie said teasingly to Devon.

"It must have been obvious that Michel was speaking for both of us," he replied smoothly.

It was a pleasant, relaxed evening. The party broke up shortly afterward, and they all went to their rooms.

Shannon had undressed and gotten into bed. Her eyelashes were drooping, but her drowsiness disappeared when the phone rang. She had a feeling it was Michel. But why was he calling when she'd just left him? Maybe he didn't want the evening to end? What would she say?

She snatched up the phone as it rang again, her pulse racing. Marcie's voice greeted her. So much for female intuition, Shannon thought sardonically.

"Wasn't I right about you and Michel?" her cousin asked. "He definitely has the hots for you."

"Is that what you called to tell me?"

"Well, I couldn't very well say it in front of him, could I?"

"I don't know how to convince you that you're way off base. Michel is a perfect gentleman. He's never said anything to me that was even the slightest bit suggestive."

"I wouldn't expect him to. He's got class."

"Then your warning—if that's what it was meant to be—is unnecessary."

"A guy can have class and still be a smooth operator. Men are all alike, whether they're princes, paupers or somewhere in between. They all want the same thing. If you had more experience, you'd know that."

"You think no man ever made a pass at me? Or that I didn't know what he had in mind? I chose not to have sex. It doesn't make me stupid," Shannon said dryly. "This is exactly why I never discussed the subject with you."

"I didn't mean to sound patronizing." Marcie tried hastily to make amends. "You've known a lot more men than I have, so of course some of them must have tried something. It's just that Michel is different. He could sweet-talk a tigress out of one of her cubs. If you really want to preserve the status quo, watch out for him."

"Thanks for your concern, but I scarcely think he'd try to seduce me here in the castle with you and Devon around."

"Maybe not, but if he suggests a moonlit walk around the grounds, watch out," Marcie said. "There's nothing more romantic than making love under the stars."

Shannon could imagine how it might happen. It would start with a fairly chaste kiss, perhaps. An expression of friendship rather than desire. But then their attraction to each other would take over, and Michel would deepen the kiss.

His hands would move over her body, lighting a slow flame. He would unzip her dress, and the sensation of his fingertips trailing tantalizingly over her bare back would fuel the fire. Then when he removed her dress and clasped her nearly nude body in his arms, she would—

"Shannon? *Shannon!* What happened to you?"

The erotic picture vanished as if a magician had waved his wand. Shannon took a deep breath to steady herself.

"Are you annoyed with me?" her cousin asked.

"No, I dozed off. Go read a book if you're at loose ends. I'm going to sleep."

Shannon hung up and turned on her stomach, burrowing her head under the pillow. She would *not* think about Michel! They were friends, nothing more, and that's the way she wanted it.

Chapter Five

Shannon was looking forward to seeing Michel in his official capacity as head of the country. In the past couple of days she'd often forgotten that he was a ruling prince. Ever since they'd overcome their original misunderstanding, he'd been such a charming companion that he seemed more like a date. The best one she'd ever had!

Oh sure, he could be somewhat autocratic at times, but not in a cutting way. Shannon had never seen a trace of meanness or pettiness in Michel.

Both princes were tied up all morning, so she and Marcie had lunch alone in the small dining room. When they went downstairs they noticed an unusual undercurrent of excitement in the air. The staff was used to guests, as visitors were part of their daily routine. Yet today they were scurrying around most uncharacteristically.

"I wonder why they're so much busier than usual," Shannon said. "I realize this awards ceremony is a big deal, but how much added work can it be? Every room in the castle always looks as if it's ready for company."

"And it isn't as if the guests are going to give the end tables the white-glove treatment," Marcie agreed. "Devon did mention that a lot of visiting royalty will be here, and of course all of their own titled gentry. Maybe that accounts for the pressure the servants are under."

"I sympathize with them, but I can't wait to get a glimpse of what royal life is really like. The ceremonial part of a monarchy, I mean."

"I just hope they don't have a lot of dull speeches like we do."

"That doesn't sound like you. You're usually willing to sit through anything, as long as it's a new experience." Shannon looked at her cousin more closely. Marcie had barely touched her quiche, which also wasn't like her. "Don't you feel well?"

"I'm fine, just a little tired. This is the first breather we've had since we left home. We've been on the go morning, noon and night. I guess I'm simply unwinding."

"I know what you mean. I slept until almost nine this morning, which is unheard-of for me. But you're the party animal in the family," Shannon laughed. "You'll bounce back as soon as the festivities begin."

"You're right, I always do." Marcie yawned and put down her fork.

"If you're finished with lunch, let's go up and start

getting ready. We have lots of time, but I'd like to get there early and watch the people arrive.''

Shannon was dressed and ready long before the appointed time for the ceremony. She had chosen a white silk suit with a wide portrait neckline that had hand-painted flowers on the lapel and waist of the short jacket.

After putting the finishing touches to her hair, she went out on the terrace. A line of cars, mostly chauffeur driven, was already snaking slowly up the long driveway.

She rushed back inside and called Marcie. A lot of other people had evidently decided to be early, too. If she and Marcie didn't get there right away they wouldn't get good seats.

The phone rang four or five times. As Shannon was about to hang up, figuring her cousin was on her way over, Marcie answered in a thick voice that didn't sound right.

"Don't tell me you went back to bed!" Shannon exclaimed.

"I lay down for just a minute and I guess I fell asleep."

"Are you at least dressed?"

"No, you'd better go without me. I don't feel so great."

Shannon was instantly concerned. "What's wrong? Do you have a temperature?"

"No, nothing like that. I just want to go back to bed."

"It's probably the best thing for you. I'll be right over."

"Don't do that, I'll be okay," Marcie assured her. "Go to the ceremony so you can tell me about it afterward."

Shannon flatly refused, but Marcie was equally insistent. Shannon finally allowed herself to be persuaded when she realized that Marcie really wanted to be alone. Before leaving the suite, however, she asked one of the servants to look in on her cousin periodically.

State affairs were conducted in a lofty hall that had tiers of seats for spectators in a balcony overlooking the lower floor. This official chamber was located in a separate wing of the castle where the business of the monarchy was conducted. It was also where the ministers and various secretaries had their offices.

Shannon had never been in that part of the castle, but she had no trouble finding it. A stream of people were walking toward a massive arched entrance where two uniformed pages were collecting engraved invitations. They directed the invited guests to seats on the ground floor, others to the balcony.

Shannon didn't recognize the pages, but there were so many people employed at the castle that it wasn't surprising. It was more important that one of them recognize *her*. Michel had neglected to give her an invitation. Fortunately it wasn't a problem.

When she reached the entry, Shannon said, "I'm a visitor here. I'm staying with—"

Before she could finish, the young man directed her to a long flight of stone steps and turned to the next person in line.

It wasn't until she had climbed to the upper gallery

that the magnificence of the vast chamber hit her. It was like something out of the Middle Ages. Scarlet, royal-blue and gold banners hung from the balcony, and flaming torches in wall sconces cast flickering light over the stone walls of the huge hall.

Facing her was a dais centered by a large, ornate throne upholstered in maroon velvet. Next to it was a slightly smaller but equally elegant throne.

Shannon was drinking in all the pageantry when an elderly woman in the front row motioned to her.

"Are you looking for a seat?" she asked. "Come sit next to me where you can see all the goings-on. Looks like my friend, Alma, isn't going to get here, so there's no sense in letting the seat I was saving go to waste."

Shannon was happy to accept. "Thank you, that's very kind of you, Mrs...."

"Call me Birdy," the woman said. "You're not from around here, are you?"

"No, I'm visiting from America." Shannon supplied her own first name.

"I'll bet you came to see our handsome prince."

"Well, not solely for that reason," Shannon smiled.

"It's nothing to be ashamed of. All the women are crazy about him."

"Yes, I can imagine," Shannon murmured.

"Not only silly young girls, mind you." Birdy wanted to be sure she understood the magnitude of Michel's attraction. "His titled lady friends are no different. The competition over him is something fierce!"

"Is there anyone who's the favorite?" Shannon asked, trying to sound only mildly interested.

"It's hard to say, but I'd guess that would be Lady Grenville. He used to be seen with her a lot." The woman leaned over the balcony to scan the crowd, then pointed to a stunning brunette in a gray suit. "That's her, the real skinny one. Whoever it's going to be, we just hope he picks a princess soon. We're ready for a wedding and a christening, even if he isn't," Birdy cackled.

Shannon was no longer listening. People were filing onto the stage. When they formed a line on either side of the throne, two liveried pages advanced to the edge of the dais and blew long golden horns. The rustling in the audience died down as Michel appeared.

Shannon scarcely recognized him. He was wearing a floor length scarlet cloak intricately embroidered with gold thread and pearls. On his head was a magnificent jeweled gold crown, and he was carrying a jeweled scepter. He looked regal and omnipotent as he gazed out at his subjects.

Devon walked behind Michel. He was wearing a less ornate cloak and a smaller crown, but he, too, looked unmistakably royal. They were totally unlike the carefree companions Shannon was used to.

When the two men were seated on their thrones, the ceremony began. One by one the honorees appeared before the throne and went down on one knee in front of Michel. He touched some on the shoulder with his scepter. Others had medals on multicolored ribbon slipped over their heads.

The last recipient hurried onstage from behind the

side draperies. Shannon was pleased to see this one was a woman, somewhere in her fifties.

She said something to Michel that made him smile. For just a moment, Shannon glimpsed the man she knew. Then he assumed his regal guise once more as he placed a medal around her neck.

"She's the only woman among the honorees," Shannon whispered to Birdy. "Is that unusual? All the rest were men."

"Well, it's a start," Birdy answered. "His Highness is the first of our rulers to include women on the honors list. If anybody deserves to be there, the duchess does. She's the angel behind a network of hospitals for the poor."

Some speeches followed the presentation, then each award winner signed a massive leather-bound book. The ceremony concluded shortly afterward, and the crowd in the balcony began to move toward the stone steps. On the ground floor, Michel was surrounded by people, while the rest of the invited guests were chatting in small groups, waiting their turn to speak to him.

As Shannon accompanied Birdy down the steps, she tried to get a closer look inside the great chamber. The tapestries on the side walls were especially intriguing.

"Get up closer to the door where you can see Prince Michel, dearie. The pages won't chase away a pretty girl like you." Birdy waved to her and merged with the departing crowd.

Shannon paused at the entry, hoping Birdy was right. It would be embarrassing to be ordered out. She heard her name called, and looked around to see Devon waving at her.

"Where have you been?" he asked when he reached her. "I looked for you and Marcie in the first row of chairs, but you weren't there. Did you get the time wrong?"

"No, I was here and I loved every minute of it." Before she could tell him about Marcie, Michel joined them.

"I thought you weren't coming," he said. "Did you just get here?"

Shannon was flattered that they had even noticed her absence. She explained that she'd actually gotten there early and was sitting upstairs in the balcony during the entire ceremony.

"Why did you go up there?" Michel asked. "I had a chair reserved for you in front of the dais."

"The pages were only admitting people in here who had an invitation, and I didn't have one."

"All you had to do was give them your name and tell them you were my guest."

She was afraid the pages might get in trouble if she told Michel they had shuttled her upstairs without giving her a chance to say anything. "It doesn't matter. I could see everything, and I was quite impressed. I don't think I'll ever be able to feel the same way about you again."

He smiled mischievously. "It would be nice to know how you felt about me before." Some people came over to talk to him and he turned away for a moment.

"Where is Marcie?" Devon asked.

"She's feeling a little under the weather," Shannon

said. "I think lack of sleep finally caught up with her."

"That's too bad. I have to hang around here for a while, but I'll try to slip out and go check on her."

"I'm sure it's nothing serious, and you have to be with your guests. I'm going to her room now to see how she's feeling."

Shannon was about to leave when Michel turned back to them. "As soon as I change out of this garb we'll go to the reception," he said.

"Why don't I meet you there?" She explained about Marcie.

After expressing his sympathy, Michel said, "The reception will be in the grand ballroom. If you have any trouble at the door, give the pages your name and tell them you're my personal guest."

"Don't worry about me. I'll speak up this time."

"You always have before," he said with amusement.

Marcie was asleep and didn't awaken when Shannon tapped lightly on the door. But her breathing was even and her forehead was fairly cool. Sleep was probably what she needed most, Shannon thought as she tiptoed out of the room.

People were streaming up the grand staircase to the ballroom on the third floor of the castle, although the reception was already in full swing, judging by the volume of noise and laughter coming from the spacious room. A string quartet was playing soft background music, undeterred by the fact that nobody was listening.

Michel was standing near the entry, surrounded by

the usual crowd of people. He had taken off his robe and crown, and was wearing one of his beautifully tailored suits. He should have looked the same to Shannon, but he didn't.

She was conscious, as never before, of the chasm that separated them. If she had ever had a romantic notion that they could be something more than friends, it had evaporated this afternoon. She had seen the real Michel, the man who was responsible for an entire country. He was a genuine prince; she was only a temporary princess.

As she stood hesitantly at the entry, he spotted her and came over to take her hand.

"I've been waiting near the door, in case you had any trouble getting in," he said. "Come, I want you to meet some of the honorees."

Shannon was always amazed by his thoughtfulness. But did he realize that people were looking curiously at them? Michel had put his arm around her shoulders to guide her through the crowd. It probably never occurred to him that people might speculate about their relationship. If he did notice, he would find it amusing.

Shannon enjoyed meeting the honorees. They were a stimulating group of people with a wide range of expertise in various fields. She especially enjoyed chatting with the duchess, who was a forceful woman with a wicked sense of humor. But the person Shannon really wanted to meet was Lady Grenville.

She got her wish when the tall, extremely thin brunette came over to link her arm through Michel's. She had long, straight black hair pulled back in a style that would have been too severe for any woman who didn't have her perfect features. She gave Shannon a cool, penetrating look before dismissing her as unimportant.

She was the first one of Michel's friends who hadn't made an effort to be gracious, but Shannon didn't let it bother her. She was just surprised that he'd be attracted to her type. Lady Grenville seemed like such a cold fish, and he was the complete opposite.

The woman's manner warmed perceptibly when she turned to Michel. "You were impressive as usual, darling, and you looked absolutely smashing!"

"Actually, the crown was giving me a headache," he answered, with a smile that included Shannon.

He introduced the two women who greeted each other politely if without enthusiasm.

Debra Grenville immediately turned back to Michel. "I want to thank you for inviting me." She made it sound as if she was a special guest. "I'm happy to know that I'm still on your list."

"The Grenville family are a fixture on the royal guest list," Michel answered smoothly.

It wasn't the answer she'd been hoping for, judging by the look on her face. Birdy was wrong. The skinny Lady Grenville wasn't in line to be Bonaventure's next princess. Shannon didn't care for her, yet she couldn't help feeling sympathetic. Michel could make a woman feel like the brightest star in his firmament, but she'd better not count on it to last.

People began to crowd around him, edging Shannon out. She realized that everyone wanted to have a word with Michel, so she went in search of Devon, the only other person there that she knew. But it was hard to find anyone in the large ballroom.

As she was scanning the crowd, a tall, genial man said, ''A pretty little lady like you can't be here all alone. Did you get separated from your boyfriend? It's no wonder with all these people.''

''It's quite a crowd, isn't it?'' Shannon smiled.

''You're an American!'' the older woman with him exclaimed. ''It's so nice to meet somebody from home.''

The man extended his hand and introduced himself as Walter Buxbaum from Texas. ''And this is my wife, Clarice. We've been touring Europe for over two weeks, and I think she's getting homesick.''

They asked where Shannon was from and chatted for a few moments about home, and how they got an invitation to today's ceremony. One of their friends knew somebody with influence in the right places.

''All the women in my bridge club are going to be green with envy when they hear we actually got inside the castle,'' Clarice said.

''I keep telling her to go say hello to the prince. That would really knock their socks off,'' Walter chuckled.

''Oh, I couldn't do that!'' she said. ''We're not really invited guests like these other people.''

''I'm sure he'd be delighted to meet you,'' Shannon said. ''He's very nice.''

''Do you know him, or did you just go up and say hello, like Walter wants me to do?''

''I've spent a little time with him.'' Shannon didn't want to get into specifics, so she said, ''I'll take you over and introduce you if you'd like.''

"Oh, I don't know. I wouldn't know what to say!" Clarice exclaimed.

"Knowing you, you'll think of something." Her husband grinned.

Michel was still surrounded, so Shannon waggled her fingers to get his attention. He excused himself immediately and came over to her.

"Where did you run off to?" he asked. "Every time I take my eyes off you, you disappear."

"You always think I'm going to get lost," she teased. "You'll have to develop more trust in me."

"It isn't a matter of trust. I just don't want to lose you."

Shannon was pleased by Michel's honeyed tone, but she didn't want the Buxbaums to get the wrong idea. They were listening avidly. "These nice people would like to meet you," she said hurriedly. "They're visiting from the United States."

Michel charmed them effortlessly. Clarice vibrated with pleasure, and even Walter was impressed. While they were chatting—giving Clarice enough ammunition to lord it over her bridge club for weeks—Shannon spotted Devon nearby. With a murmured excuse, she went over to join him.

"I went down to check on Marcie," he said, before Shannon could ask.

"Was she awake?"

"Yes, but she doesn't feel too great."

"I'll go down there right now," Shannon fretted.

"The doctor said it was nothing serious. She—"

"You called the doctor?" Now Shannon was really concerned.

"Just to be on the safe side. Besides, he was right here at the reception."

"What did he say? What's wrong with her?"

"He says it's a touch of intestinal flu, nothing to worry about. It only lasts a couple of days. Fortunately doctors never go anywhere without their little black bags. Mac's was in his car. He gave her some pills to take care of the headache and queasy feeling."

"I'm glad it's not serious, but poor Marcie. She'll hate giving up two days of her vacation."

"The rest will do her good," Devon said. "I'll get a television set and a VCR sent up to her room so she can watch movies. She'll be up and around before you know it."

"You're a very nice man." Shannon patted his arm.

"Hey, what are friends for?"

"You and Michel are the greatest," she said. "If he looks for me, tell him I'm sorry I ran out on him again, and I hope the Buxbaums didn't talk his ear off."

"Who are the Buxbaums?"

Shannon laughed. "Michel will be able to tell you their entire family history."

Marcie looked rather wan, but she mustered a smile for Shannon. "How was the awards ceremony? Tell me every single detail."

"It was great, and when you're up to it, I'll tell you what all the women were wearing. Right now, I want to know how you feel."

"Kind of lousy, but the doctor says I'll feel better

in the morning. Did you know that Devon called his own private physician for me?''

"Yes, he told me. Was the doctor properly reverential, or do only the princes get that treatment?" Shannon joked.

"He's a great guy, but I wish he'd lighten up a little. He told me I had to stay in bed today and tomorrow. What a waste of time!"

"It won't be so bad. Devon is going to get you a television set. We'll lie around and watch movies and ask the kitchen to send up ice cream and custard. Those go down easily.''

"You're not going to waste your whole day sitting here with me,'' Marcie said firmly.

"I don't have anything else to do. Michel and Devon are going to a wedding, remember?''

"You could find something more interesting than baby-sitting. Why don't you go with them?''

"It's polite to wait until you're asked,'' Shannon said.

"You could drop a few hints. This is just too good to miss. When will you ever get another chance to go to a royal wedding?''

"I was only kidding. I wouldn't leave you here alone, you know that.''

They argued the point back and forth. Finally Shannon agreed to go if Michel invited her, knowing he wouldn't.

After the reception ended, both princes came to see how Marcie was feeling. Michel had stuffed his tie in his pocket and unfastened several buttons of his white dress shirt. He was sprawled in an armchair with his long legs stretched out and crossed at the ankles.

"Ahh, this is better." He sighed contentedly.

"I was hoping you'd be wearing your red velvet cloak and your jeweled crown," Marcie teased. "I missed out on seeing them."

"I'll give you one of the photos that Shannon's friends, the Buxbaums, snapped at the ceremony. They took enough pictures to fill *People Magazine*." He sounded amused, rather than annoyed.

"Sorry about that," Shannon said. "They were so thrilled at the chance to actually speak to you, that I couldn't resist. I suppose it seems trivial to you, but a lot of people are fascinated by royalty."

"Like us," Marcie said. "I'll bet just about everybody at your cousin's wedding will have a title. Shannon would—"

Before she could finish, Shannon stuck a thermometer in her mouth. "It's time to take your temperature again. I know it'll be difficult for you, but you have to keep your mouth closed." She gave Marcie a meaningful look.

Devon laughed. "That's a lot to ask, even in her weakened condition."

To Shannon's relief, Michel stood and said, "Come on, Devon, we don't want to tire her out. Feel better, Marcie, and if there is anything you want or need, just ring for it."

Devon followed his brother to the door. "Mac said those pills would make her sleepy," he said to Shannon. "So if you want to come down and have a drink before dinner, we'll be in the den."

She stayed for another half hour, until Marcie's eyelids started to droop again. Then Shannon went to her suite to change out of the clothes she'd worn all afternoon.

Since they weren't going out that evening, she changed into slim white pants and a white silk blouse printed with large red poppies. She tied the ends of the shirt at her waist for a casual look.

When Shannon joined the two men in the den, both Michel and Devon stood, as they always did when she entered a room. It was a gesture of old-world courtesy that she found charming. Their unfailing compliments on her appearance—no matter what she was wearing—were also gratifying.

While they were discussing the reception, Shannon remarked artlessly, "Everybody looked lovely today, of course, but I thought Lady Grenville was especially stunning."

"She rarely gets a compliment from another woman." Devon shot an amused look at his brother. "The infighting over His Highness here can get downright ugly."

"Devon is doing what he does best, being annoying," Michel said. "Don't pay any attention to him. Debra is simply an old friend."

Shannon was gratified to hear it. She doubted that Lady Grenville had always fit that category, but she was yesterday's news. That was what counted.

Michel changed the subject. "I think we should leave by early afternoon tomorrow, Devon. Say, about two o'clock."

"It's just a short flight," his brother objected. "And the festivities don't start until evening."

"I know, but we haven't spent any time with the family lately."

"That's because Great-Aunt Sophie drives you up the wall." Devon mimicked his aunt's falsetto. "'When are you boys going to get married? The suitable girls aren't going to wait forever, you know.'"

"Thanks for reminding me." Michel laughed. "We'll leave at five. Tell Stefan to have the plane ready."

"Do you have your own airplane?" Shannon asked.

He nodded. "It's more convenient than being restricted by airline schedules. Especially on a short hop like this one to Cap d'Antibes. We can come and go as we please."

"It sounds like the ultimate luxury to me. A private plane *and* the Riviera. Is it as glamorous as it looks in the travel brochures?"

"Haven't you ever been there?"

"No, this is my first trip to Europe, remember?"

"You really should see some of the Continent while you're here. I have a suggestion. Why don't you come with us tomorrow?"

"I wasn't hinting," Shannon protested. Marcie would have been proud of her, she thought ruefully.

"I didn't think you were, but it's still a good idea. It will only be a short trip, but at least you'll get a glimpse of the South of France."

"That's very thoughtful of you, but I couldn't leave Marcie while she's sick."

"I wouldn't want you to if she were seriously ill. The doctor says it's just a minor upset. He'll be here if she needs him, and we won't be that far away. So, come with us.'' When Shannon looked doubtful, Michel said, ''I'll tell you what. Ask Marcie. If she wants you to stay with her, I'll understand.''

''She already told me she didn't want me to sit in her room all day. But that's not my only reason for turning down your nice invitation. You're going to a wedding and I'm not invited.''

''No problem,'' Michel assured her. ''I'll call tonight and tell my family that I'm bringing a guest. They'll be delighted to meet you.''

''Especially Aunt Sophie.'' Devon grinned. ''Be prepared for an interrogation worthy of the Spanish Inquisition,'' he warned Shannon.

''Don't let Devon scare you off,'' Michel said. ''There's always the chance that she'll be on her good behavior.''

''I do remember that happening once—back in 1986, I believe,'' Devon remarked.

Chapter Six

Shannon had expected Michel's plane to be one of the small, brightly painted kind that almost looked like overgrown toys. Instead, the silver twin-engine jet waiting in a private area of the airport was the sort used by corporations to fly their CEOs around the world.

The interior looked almost like a living room, with couches, comfortable chairs and a standing card table. At the back of the plane was a bedroom. It wasn't spacious by the castle's standards, but it was large enough for an oversize bed, a chest of drawers and a dressing table. A door led to one of the two bathrooms on board. The other was in the front of the plane, along with a compact galley.

Shannon went around inspecting everything, but when they flew over the Riviera, her nose was pressed to a window.

"I've never seen water that blue!" she exclaimed. "And the foam edging those long waves looks like lace on the hem of a silk gown."

Michel smiled indulgently. "I thought you'd enjoy seeing it."

"Oh, look, we're coming to a city. There's a cruise ship in the harbor."

He leaned over to look out the window. "That's not a liner, it's a private yacht."

"It can't be, it's huge!"

Michel knelt on the couch next to her. "The Mediterranean is full of yachts that size. I can't be sure from this distance, but it probably belongs to a Greek shipping magnate. He spends a lot of time in Monaco. That's Monte Carlo overlooking the harbor."

Shannon shifted her gaze to the alluring little city. The steep hills overlooking the wide beach were covered with houses that clung to the slopes, seemingly defying the laws of gravity.

"Is that a castle over there on top of that hill?" she asked. "I see men in uniform out front. I guess they're guards. They look like toy soldiers from here."

Michel put his arm around her shoulder and leaned in closer for a better look. "That's Prince Rainier's palace."

"I should have guessed. It looks elegant, just the way I pictured it." She sighed happily.

As the plane continued on, leaving Monte Carlo behind, Shannon turned her head for a last glimpse. When the city was out of sight she realized that her face was only inches from Michel's. His arm tightened and his head dipped ever so slightly toward hers.

They stared into each other's eyes for a long moment before she summoned the willpower to move back.

"That was very exciting. Seeing Monte Carlo, I mean," she added a little breathlessly.

"Yes, I knew what you meant," he answered, trying not to smile.

Why couldn't she match Michel's sophistication? Shannon thought despairingly. Even if he had kissed her, it wouldn't have been a big deal. Especially with Devon sprawled in a chair a few feet away, reading a newspaper.

It wasn't as if she was inexperienced with men; she'd certainly dated enough of them. Some of the men she'd gone with had been successful, polished executives, and she hadn't felt awkward with them. Was it because Michel was a prince? That was the easy answer. But Shannon had a feeling her tension was due to the undercurrent of mutual sexual attraction that was always present between them.

The panorama unfolding below them distracted her as their plane slowly descended, preparatory to landing. The beachfront houses grew larger, and she could see people sitting under umbrellas on the sand.

A car was waiting for them when they got off the plane, but it wasn't a limousine, which Shannon would have expected. It was a shiny red sports car.

Michel glanced at his watch and said, "Good, we're right on schedule. We'll have plenty of time for a drive and some sight-seeing."

"But the car is a two-seater," Shannon said. "We won't all fit in."

"I'm spending the afternoon with friends," Devon

explained. "They'll be here any minute, so you two don't have to wait around."

"Don't be late," Michel warned as he opened the car door for Shannon. "Aunt Sophie will want to know where you've been."

"She will anyway," Devon said. "Be sure and drive Shannon through Juan-les-Pins."

"What's special about it?" she asked as they drove away.

"Devon likes it because it's a party town, with lots of bars and nightclubs. Back in the 1930s, before casinos were commonplace, the one in Juan-les-Pins was a magnet for celebrities. One of them was Coco Chanel, the famous couturiere, who was refused entrance because she was wearing something called beach pajamas. They were the new craze at the time, but evidently the doorman wasn't fashion conscious."

"It seems laughable that she would be turned away for something like that, considering what women wear to the beach nowadays."

"Or don't wear," Michel said. "Topless beaches are the norm on the Riviera."

"So I've heard," Shannon answered briefly.

He slanted an amused glance at her. "You don't approve? It's supposed to be quite healthy."

"Whatever." She turned her head to look out the side window at the sapphire-blue sea and the surf gently breaking against the shore. "The water looks so inviting. I wish we could go swimming."

"How badly do you want to?" His gray eyes sparkled with mischief. "If I remember correctly, there's a nude beach just up the road a bit."

Shannon knew he was only teasing. He expected

her to blush and get flustered the way she did all too often with him. Well, this time he was due for a surprise.

"That sounds cool," she remarked. "No pun intended. I'm game if you are."

"How could I turn down such an enchanting prospect?" He smiled and stepped on the gas pedal.

The powerful sports car zoomed down the highway. In just a few minutes Michel pulled off the road and parked in front of a broad, deserted strip of beach.

"Here we are," he said, getting out of the car and coming around to her side. "It looks like we have the beach all to ourselves today. Isn't that great?"

"I can't believe we could be so lucky."

Shannon took the hand he extended, because she didn't know what else to do. She certainly wasn't going skinny-dipping with him, but if he was only playing a game of chicken with her, she didn't want to be the one to squawk first!

"Look for a rock to anchor our clothes so they don't blow away," he said, as they strolled onto the sand. "I can't wait to feel that cool water on my bare skin. This was a great idea you had."

"Yes, well…"

As she scrambled for some way to back out and still save face, they rounded a large boulder and saw some other people on the beach. One couple was lying on a blanket, the others were sitting on the sand or strolling along the shore. All of them were wearing bathing suits.

Shannon looked at Michel indignantly. "You knew this wasn't a nude beach! How long were you going to let this practical joke go on? What if I'd taken off my clothes before I realized it?''

''I would have been incredibly grateful,'' he chuckled. When he saw that she was really annoyed, he said, ''I knew there was no chance of that. You got embarrassed when I caught one quick glimpse of you, partially nude. You weren't going to suddenly change into a free spirit who would fling her clothes off in public.''

''If you knew that, you could have been a good sport and blinked first,'' she muttered.

''All right, I owe you one.'' He put an arm around her shoulders and hugged her against his hard body. ''Are we friends again?''

As she looked up into his handsome, laughing face, her annoyance evaporated. ''Okay, but only because I don't believe in holding grudges.''

He kissed her on the cheek and said, ''I always knew you were a saint.''

Shannon didn't feel like one. Under the right circumstances—such as if the beach was deserted and lit only by moonlight—it was conceivable that she could be a sinner.

They strolled along the beach, hand in hand, stopping now and then to pick up pretty or unusual seashells. Shannon could have spent the entire day just having Michel all to herself. He seemed to enjoy her company, too, but he was the one who suggested they continue their drive.

''I want you to see some of the little towns along the coast before we have to start back,'' he said.

Shannon had to admit the scenic drive was spectacular. The lovely houses along the waterfront sometimes blocked the view of the sea, but the beautiful flowers and greenery were a different kind of treat.

Cap d'Antibes seemed larger, and definitely more luxurious than any place they'd driven through. It was the site of the famous Eden Roc Hotel, often described as the most fabulous hotel in the world.

"A roster of their guests reads like a Who's Who of the world," Michel told Shannon. "Everyone from foreign princes, heads of state and stars from the entertainment field have stayed there. It's a very luxurious hotel, but they have one odd little quirk. Credit cards aren't accepted, only cash."

"That's almost unheard-of nowadays! Especially considering what their prices must be. How can anybody carry around that much money?"

"And you thought the rich didn't have problems," he teased.

A short distance from the hotel, the road was bordered by high walls broken occasionally by gates. Before Shannon could ask what was behind the walls, Michel drove through one of the entrances and she could see for herself.

Inside the gates, which were monitored by security cameras, there were opulent mansions surrounded by extensive grounds. The road wound past one vast estate after another.

Michel turned into a driveway leading to a huge, sprawling pink villa whose walls were blanketed with scarlet bougainvillea. "Here we are, with plenty of time to change," he said as they walked to the front door. Michel had arranged for them to change into their evening clothes at his Aunt Celeste's villa.

A uniformed maid admitted them and greeted

Michel with smiling deference. "The family are all in the drawing room, your highness."

"Thank you, Rosa. It's nice to see you again."

While he gave the maid their hand luggage, Shannon looked around the large foyer. The marble floor and Venetian chandelier hanging over a marquetry table, were undoubtedly a foretaste of the elegance to be found in the rest of the house.

When the maid had left, he said to Shannon, "We'll just pop in for a minute and tell them we're here. Are you ready to meet Aunt Sophie?"

"I'd prefer to change clothes first," Shannon said. "She might not approve of my outfit."

"I'm wearing jeans, too."

"That's different. You're a prince."

"And you're a princess."

"Not a real one."

"I don't know of another princess who is as genuine as you are." Michel cupped her chin in his palm and raised her face to his. "You're very sweet."

"That's a nice compliment," she murmured.

Their faces were so close that she could see each spiky black lash that fringed his gray eyes. When her lips parted unconsciously, his head dipped slowly toward hers.

"Well, I must say, this looks promising." A woman's voice penetrated their secret world, causing them to draw apart self-consciously. "Is there finally going to be an announcement?"

Michel recovered his poise immediately. He kissed his aunt on the cheek and—sidestepping the question—told her how happy he was to see her. Then he introduced the two women.

Great-Aunt Sophie was elderly, but by no means infirm. She was a tall woman with perfectly styled silver hair and erect posture. Shannon had a feeling the cane she carried was more for authority than any real need. Her dark eyes moved from her nephew to Shannon with lively curiosity.

"Why haven't I met this young lady before?" she demanded. "You're obviously close friends."

"I'd be honored to have Shannon consider me her friend," Michel answered smoothly.

"Don't use that social mumbo jumbo on me," his aunt said disgustedly. She turned to Shannon as a more likely source of information. "I don't recognize the name Blanchard. Where are you from? Who are your parents?"

"I'm afraid you wouldn't know them, either," Shannon said. "I'm not a native of your country."

"Shannon is visiting from America," Michel explained.

Aunt Sophie frowned. "America? That's the country that caused England so much inconvenience."

"It was a long time ago." Shannon's eyes sparkled with suppressed laughter. "Our countries are very good friends now."

"Yes, well, I suppose one must rise above these things."

"It's wonderful to see you again, Aunt Sophie. If you'll excuse us now, we have to change for the wedding," Michel said, before she could resume her interrogation. "We'll see you later."

"You have plenty of time. I want to find out more about your young lady."

A stunning woman in a beautiful beaded gown

started across the entry, creating a welcome diversion. She stopped and held out her arms when she saw Michel. "Darling! We've all been waiting eagerly for you. It's been so long since we've seen you."

"Much too long," he agreed. "This is my Aunt Celeste, the mother of the bride," he told Shannon.

"It's so nice of you to make room for me at the last minute like this," Shannon said. "I hope I didn't inconvenience you."

"Not at all, my dear. I'm very happy you could come."

"I gave our garment bags to Rosa," Michel said. "Is there someplace we can change clothes for tonight?"

"Of course. The house is overflowing a bit at the moment, but you can use Leonard's study. I'll tell Rosa to bring your things up there."

As the three of them started toward the staircase, Great Aunt Sophie complained, "Do you all intend to run off and desert me?"

Michel gave a sigh of relief when the front door opened and his brother appeared. "Here's Devon. You can visit with him until we get back."

"Thanks a lot," Devon muttered.

"This will teach you not to be late," Michel grinned.

When Shannon realized that she and Michel were both supposed to change clothes in his uncle's study, she tried to be adult about it. They certainly couldn't expect two separate rooms. The extensive wedding party was already filling all the guest rooms to capacity, as the eight bridesmaids and an equal number of groomsmen got ready for the big event.

Michel didn't seem aware of the intimate situation. "I'm going to take a quick shower," he said. "Unless you'd like to take one."

"I showered right before we left." It occurred to her that she could slip into her gown while he was in the bathroom. "I'll just get dressed."

"Don't rush. I'll warn you when I'm ready to come out." From the amused look on his face, Shannon realized he'd guessed her dilemma.

Their garment bags and Shannon's cosmetic case were delivered promptly, so she was able to do a quick repair job to her makeup as well. She was zipping up her gown when he turned off the shower.

A few moments later, Michel called through the door, "Will you hand me my garment bag?"

As she carried it over to the bathroom, he opened the door. He had a towel wrapped around his hips, and a few drops of water glistened on his broad, tanned chest. Shannon tried not to stare, but it was hard not to.

"Do I pass inspection?" he chuckled.

She felt her cheeks grow warm, but she kept her voice as light as his. "If you're asking for my opinion, you're in great shape."

"That's very flattering—depending on how many men I'm competing against."

"I'd need time to count them all."

He laughed. "For someone with that much experience, you seem remarkably innocent."

"I'm just reticent. You don't talk about *your* love life."

"Touché!" He took the garment bag she was still holding. "All right, I won't tease you anymore."

When Michel came out of the bathroom, he was wearing black tuxedo trousers and a formal pleated white shirt. As he was fastening his cuff links, he took a better look at Shannon.

"You look absolutely ravishing! You're going to outshine the bride."

"Nobody does that. Even homely brides are beautiful on their wedding days." She smoothed her full skirt.

Shannon was wearing a sea-foam-green chiffon gown that had a Grecian-style wrapped bodice. It was held up by a fold of the same chiffon, draped diagonally across one shoulder.

"I can just imagine what a breathtaking bride you're going to be," he said.

"Can you tell me what the groom looks like? I haven't been able to picture him."

"He'll be a very lucky man, whoever he is," Michel said in a husky voice.

Shannon gazed into his brilliant eyes for a long moment before shaking off his spell. "See? You can't picture him, either."

Michel's relatives and some close friends were gathered in one of the large drawing rooms, bringing each other up-to-date on the latest family news. When Michel introduced Shannon, she could see the speculation in their eyes, but they were too well-bred to grill her as Aunt Sophie had.

Shannon found it easy to talk to Michel's cousins, some of whom were about her age. They weren't the least bit condescending when they found out she worked for a living. In fact, they were fascinated by her profession and asked a lot of questions.

"I think you're so admirable," Mimi commented. "A woman *should* be able to support herself."

"I agree," said Yvette, another of the cousins. "What would you and I do if we had to fend for ourselves?"

"You'd manage," Shannon said. "It's surprising how resourceful necessity can make you."

"Perhaps, but I'm going to see to it that my children—whether they're boys or girls—are trained to make a living."

Yvette was engaged and planned to be married in the fall. Devon joined them as she was showing off her eye-popping diamond engagement ring.

"This is the last family wedding I'm attending," he declared. "They bring out the nesting impulse in otherwise normal people."

Mimi gave him a mischievous grin. "Has somebody been asking you when you intend to get married?"

"Somebody? How about everybody? Why is a bachelor an affront to all of our female relatives?"

"Not all of us, only Aunt Sophie."

"No, you're all matchmakers at heart," Devon said.

"We have to be. Men would never get married unless they were shamed, flattered or coerced into it," Yvette told him. "And then the species would die out."

"Which method did you use to land Raoul?" he joked.

Michel's family members all clamored for his attention, but he came over several times to see that Shannon wasn't neglected. Once he saw that she was enjoying herself, he gave her a smile, said a few words and left again.

But when Leonard, the father of the bride, announced that their presence was requested in the garden in fifteen minutes, Shannon couldn't see Michel anywhere in the crowded room. She decided to check her hair and makeup before the wedding. As she approached the open door to the powder room, she heard Mimi and Yvette talking about her.

"What do you think of Shannon?"

"I really like her. She's not only beautiful, but extremely bright."

"I meant, for Michel. He certainly seems taken with her. Do you think he's serious this time?"

"Shannon would be perfect for him, but you know how Michel is. He can make a woman believe she's the center of his universe, but it never seems to last. For him, anyway."

"I know what you mean. Remember the—"

Shannon didn't wait to hear any more. She turned and walked back to the drawing room. She hadn't meant to eavesdrop, but it was a lucky accident. Michel's cousins had confirmed what Shannon already knew in her heart—he was a charmer who shouldn't be taken seriously. If she were ever tempted to believe she was different from all the rest, this overheard conversation would be a reminder.

Michel was searching the room when she returned. "I've been looking all over for you," he said. "I thought you'd deserted me."

"You should have known I wouldn't leave you." When his eyes started to glow, she added, "How would I get back to Bonaventure?"

He laughed and put his arm around her shoulders, walking her toward the French doors that led to the terrace. "You're not very good for my ego."

"At least you know where you stand with me," she answered, a trifle tartly.

"Do I?" He gazed at her appraisingly. "You send out mixed signals. Sometimes I wonder if I really know you."

Ushers were waiting on the terrace to seat the guests. One of the young men approached Michel and said, "This way, your highness." He led them to seats right in front.

The huge backyard was filled with rows of little gold chairs arranged in a semicircle around a gold carpet. Velvet ropes cordoning off the aisle were looped between posts topped with magnificent floral arrangements. Lilies speckled with scarlet were interspersed among white roses and fragrant gardenias, which perfumed the garden.

Shannon inhaled and said happily, "This must be what heaven smells like."

"Take a deep breath, Michel—just in case we don't make it through the gates," Devon said. He was seated on her other side.

"Shannon will put in a good word for us." Michel gave her a melting smile, which she returned.

She had decided to enjoy being the palace favorite while she had the chance. After all, how emotionally involved could she get in just two weeks?

Musicians at one end of the terrace began to play

softly, and the buzz of conversation died down. Everybody's attention was focused on the stately procession of bridesmaids and groomsmen who paced slowly toward a flower-bedecked g~~ ~ho at the end of the aisle.

Women in the audience murmured approval over the bridesmaids' filmy lavender dresses and bouquets of purple orchids tied with matching satin ribbons. They were followed by the maid of honor and the best man, who came in for their share of admiration. It was a long procession, due to the size of the wedding party.

Anticipation built for the long-awaited arrival of the bride. When she appeared on the arm of her proud father, a collective sigh of happiness rippled through the guests.

"She's so beautiful," Shannon whispered.

"You said all brides are beautiful," Michel teased.

"Not like this."

Bettina's wedding gown had clearly been made by a famous couturier. It had a long train and an intricately styled bodice that could only have been designed by an expert. She carried a charming bouquet of white orchids and lily of the valley, circled by white satin bows with long streamers.

Shannon listened to the wedding ceremony with rapt attention, unaware of Michel's bemused eyes on her face. When the rites were over and the groom had kissed his bride, Shannon's eyes were misty.

"Why do women always cry at weddings?" Michel asked, handing her a clean white handkerchief.

"I guess because we aren't afraid to show our emotions,'' she said, dabbing at her eyes. ''Men think it's unmanly.''

''I don't agree. Men can get very emotional, under the right circumstances.''

''Passion doesn't count,'' she said dryly.

''Don't knock it until you've tried it,'' he teased.

They were soon surrounded by people commenting on the beautiful ceremony. As the guests stood around in groups talking, servants were busy removing the rows of chairs and placing them around tables covered with gold tablecloths.

Night had fallen and the grounds looked like a scene from fairyland. Candles twinkled on every table, and tall torches were spaced at intervals around the lawn. The orchestra played softly, providing a pleasant backdrop to the voices and laughter of the crowd.

A dance floor had been laid on the grass, and a few couples circled the floor. But most of the guests were drinking champagne and greeting each other before dinner was served.

''This has been the most wonderful day,'' Shannon remarked to Michel when they were alone for a few moments. ''I wish it didn't have to end.''

''Everything ends sooner or later, but perhaps we can prolong this evening. Would you like to stop in at the casino after dinner?''

''Could we?''

He smiled at her eager expression. ''We can do anything you like. That's the fun of being a princess.''

Devon joined them, looking restless. ''I hope there aren't too many toasts to the happy couple. I'd like to take off right after dinner.''

"Sorry to disappoint you, but Shannon and I are going to the casino from here. We won't be leaving for home until around midnight."

"Then I think I'll hitch a ride on the Blenvilles' plane. They only brought one other couple, so I'm sure there's room for me." Devon left to look for his friends.

The dinner was elegant, with course after course of delicious food. There were also numerous toasts, and Shannon had to agree with Devon. She was eager to go on to the next experience.

The casino was totally unlike the ones in Las Vegas that Shannon was used to. Those were noisy and crowded with people wearing ultracasual clothes.

The atmosphere at the casino in Cap d'Antibes was restrained, and many of the people were in evening clothes, like Shannon and Michel. All the women wore high style, expensive dresses, and the men had on suits or dinner jackets.

Michel gave Shannon a stack of chips and asked what she wanted to play. She wasn't too knowledgeable about gambling and there weren't any slot machines, so she chose to sit beside him while he played a game called chemin de fer.

When Michel could see that it was a complete mystery to her, he was planning to cash in his chips and take her to the bar. Shannon was enjoying just being there. But since he wouldn't believe that, she told him to stay where he was as she had decided to play roulette. After all, how hard could it be, she reasoned. You put a chip on a number and hoped the wheel would stop there.

The people all around her were putting multiple chips in perplexing places, not squarely on a number. Shannon was reluctant to get in their way so she waited. When the croupier looked at her questioningly, with his hand on the wheel, she reached out hesitantly and placed one chip on number twenty-eight, her age.

A distinguished looking man next to her smiled. "Is this your first time here?"

"Yes," she admitted. "Did I do something wrong already?"

The beautifully groomed older woman with him said, "Not at all, my dear. Play however you like and enjoy yourself."

The little silver ball had been rattling around in the spinning wheel, which now slowed to a stop. The ball made a final lurch and dropped into number twenty-eight.

"I won!" Shannon exclaimed in delight as the croupier added tall stacks of chips to her single one.

"You can teach us how to play," the man laughed.

She wasn't as successful on the next few spins. "I guess it was beginner's luck," she sighed.

A man across the table told her, "You could increase your chance of winning if you played the corners."

"Or even black or red," somebody else said.

Soon everybody at the table was helping her, and her pile of chips grew modestly.

Michel came over several times to make sure she was having a good time. He watched her indulgently for a few moments, but Shannon was so absorbed she wasn't even aware of him.

Sometime after midnight he returned and said, "I'm sorry to drag you away, but I'm afraid we have to leave. I'll cash in your chips for you."

She couldn't believe what time it was. "I had no idea it was this late!"

"That means you were having fun, which was the whole idea." He accepted a sheaf of bills from the cashier and handed them to Shannon. "You did very well. Here are your winnings."

She didn't want to take them, saying it was his money since he had bought her first stack of chips. They argued about it all the way back to the airport. Finally Michel reluctantly agreed to accept his original stake, since she wouldn't agree to anything else.

Shannon looked at the unfamiliar bills and asked, "How much is this?" When he told her, she gasped. "How much was each chip worth?"

"In American money? About a hundred dollars," he said dismissively.

"Why didn't you tell me?" she demanded. "You must have known I wouldn't bet that kind of money."

"That's why I didn't tell you," he said with a grin.

They had arrived at the airport, where it was almost like getting into a taxi. As soon as their luggage was brought aboard, the engines roared to life and they thundered down the runway.

Shannon gazed out the window at the same scenery that had enthralled her on the trip over. It was even more beautiful at night. They were surrounded by little winking lights—those of the small resorts on the ground and the stars in the sky above.

In spite of the gorgeous vista, Shannon's eyelids started to droop after a short time. It had been a long and eventful day. Her cheek gradually came to rest against the windowpane.

Michel was standing at the card table, rummaging through his attaché case. "I'll be with you in a moment. I just want to check for some documents I'll need in the morning."

When she didn't answer, he glanced over at her. He smiled fondly when he saw she had fallen asleep. He walked over and lifted her into his arms.

She opened her eyes and said, "What are you doing?"

"Shh, go back to sleep." Michel smothered his laughter as he imagined her reaction if he'd told her he was taking her to bed. Instead, he said, "I'm just going to make you more comfortable."

"Oh." Her lashes fanned her cheeks once more.

She looped an arm around his neck and rested her head on his shoulder while he carried her into the bedroom.

Michel stood beside the bed and gazed at her for a long moment before settling her among the pillows. But when he started to straighten up, Shannon's arm tightened around his neck.

He knelt beside the bed and stroked her cheek gently, murmuring, "I wish this was what you wanted, little angel."

With a sigh, he leaned forward and touched his lips to hers. It was a mere whisper of a kiss, but Shannon made a small sound of contentment. Michel lifted his head, eyes brilliant with anticipation. The light died when he saw that she was still asleep.

He carefully disengaged her arms, covered her with a fleecy throw and walked out of the room.

Chapter Seven

Shannon didn't remember much about the plane ride home when she awoke in her bedroom at the castle the next morning. But every other detail of her glorious visit to the Riviera came rushing back to her.

What a thoughtful, generous man he was! Michel had devoted the entire time to making sure she enjoyed herself—almost as if he really cared about her. Then Shannon remembered the overheard conversation between his cousins and the fact that no relationship seemed to last for him.

But so what? She didn't expect it to. She was getting more out of their relationship than he was. Shannon was embarrassed to remember that she had slept most of the way home on the plane ride, leaving Michel to amuse himself. Some jet-setter *she* was!

Little flashes of memory started coming back to

her. Michel carrying her into the bedroom, covering her with a mohair throw. But there was something else. Had he kissed her—or was that a dream? Had she just imagined his lips touching hers? He had said something to her, too. But what? It seemed important to remember.

The bedside phone rang, startling her and dissipating the wisps of memory.

"I thought you'd call me this morning," Marcie complained. "I waited as long as I could."

"What time is it?" Shannon looked at the clock and gasped. "Would you believe I'm still in bed?"

"Alone?"

"Of course alone! Michel is a perfect gentleman."

"Too bad," Marcie laughed. "Did you have a good time?"

"I had an absolutely glorious time!"

"I want to hear every single detail. I'm all dressed, so I'll come to your suite. We can decide what we want to do after you tell me about the Riviera."

"How do you feel?" Shannon asked belatedly.

"All better and rarin' to go."

"I think you should take it easy for one more day, just to play it safe. We don't have anything planned, anyway. Michel will be in meetings all day, and Devon will be with him."

"I feel fine. I'm not going to waste the whole day sitting around the castle." Marcie had to laugh when she realized how incongruous that sounded. "What I mean is, we don't really need the guys. Let's take a car and a driver and go someplace."

"Okay, if you're sure you're up to it. I'll take a quick shower."

Shannon was in the dressing room, selecting an outfit for the day, when the phone rang once more. Her pulse quickened as she ran into the bedroom. It could only be Michel.

But it was Marcie instead. "I forgot to ask what you're going to wear."

Disappointment made Shannon's voice sharper than she intended. "What difference does it make?" She was instantly sorry and hastened to make amends. "I think I'll wear a skirt today. Why don't you wear that cute blue-and-white outfit you got on sale?"

After they had discussed it and hung up, Shannon stripped off her nightgown and started toward the bathroom. The phone rang again, but this time she wasn't foolish enough to expect to hear from Michel. If Marcie didn't stop calling, though, they'd never get out of here!

Snatching up the phone, she said, "Make it fast. I'm standing here naked."

There was a moment's silence. Then Michel's deep, rich chuckle sent a ripple down her spine. "If that's an invitation, I'll be right over."

"I didn't know it was…I mean, I thought you were…" She took a deep breath to make herself stop babbling. "Marcie has been phoning every five minutes, and I've been trying to take a shower."

"Then I won't keep you."

"Oh, no, it's all right! I'm glad you called. I want to thank you for a wonderful time yesterday. I would have called *you,* but I thought you'd be tied up all day."

"I will be, unfortunately. I just gave everyone a

short break. I wanted to see how you're feeling this morning. You were so tired last night.''

''I have to apologize for falling asleep on you. I'm so sorry.''

''Don't be. I enjoyed watching you.'' His voice was like plush velvet. ''You sleep the way you do everything else, very gracefully.''

''That's very flattering.''

''I'm sure I'm not the first man to tell you that.''

''Well, um…'' Shannon scrambled for some way to change the subject. When nothing came to mind, she said abruptly, ''Marcie and I are going to borrow a car and driver today. I hope that's all right.''

''Of course. I'm sorry I won't be able to join you, but we'll make up for it tomorrow. I'll let you go now.'' Laughter filled his voice once more. ''I need time to shake off the mental picture of you in the nude before I go back to my meeting.''

After they'd hung up, Shannon told herself that Michel had just been teasing her. Not that he'd turn down an opportunity to have sex if he thought she was willing. He was a man, after all! But he would never pressure her, or become annoyed that she wasn't more receptive. Actually it was a mark of their growing friendship that Michel could joke about the fact that they *weren't* sleeping together.

By the time Marcie arrived and they'd discussed everything that had gone on the day before, Shannon felt good about their relationship.

At breakfast the next morning, Devon said, ''I'll bet you two had a better time yesterday than Michel and I did.''

"Devon is annoyed that work got in the way of his playtime," Michel said dryly.

"I intend to make up for it today. The curator of the Royal Museum left me a message. He has arranged a private showing of the crown jewels for this afternoon."

"How neat!" Marcie exclaimed.

"That still leaves us all morning," Michel said. "I promised Shannon I'd take her to the flea market. If you still want to go, that is." He looked at her inquiringly.

"Oh, yes! I didn't think you remembered."

"I never forget a promise." He gave her a warm smile before turning to the others. "You and Marcie are welcome to join us."

Devon answered for both of them. "It gets confusing if there are too many of us. Some want to linger, and others don't. Marcie and I will go exploring on our own."

"That might be best," Michel agreed rapidly. "We'll meet you at the museum then."

The flea market was held on the outskirts of town in a large field. It looked much like outdoor marts all over the world. Rickety stalls were lined up along makeshift streets, and merchandise was displayed on card tables, or spilled out of cartons that customers rummaged through, looking for buried treasure.

In a separate area, vendors had a variety of snacks for sale, but they were very different from the mundane selection of hot dogs and pizza back home. One stand sold crepes sprinkled with powdered sugar and some kind of orange sauce. They came in a little square cardboard container, complete with a plastic fork.

Another stand displayed appetizing-looking shish kebabs on long bamboo skewers. Even in the middle of the morning, people were wandering from stand to stand, eating the grilled chunks of meat and vegetables from the slender stick.

"Do you see anything that appeals to you?" Michel asked.

Shannon shook her head. "It all looks delicious, but we just finished breakfast."

"How about a Belgian waffle?" he coaxed, gesturing toward a stand that had a display of golden fluted waffles topped with whipped cream and strawberries.

She shook her head reluctantly. "I know I'll be sorry I didn't try one, but I'm still full from breakfast."

"We'll shop around for a while. You might change your mind."

They browsed through the stands, drifting from one to the next. Most of the merchandise was uninspired or touristy. There were the usual ashtrays and plates with Bonaventure and a scene of the castle painted on them. There was also a lot of inexpensive costume jewelry. The items popular with tourists were anything depicting a crown, either made into pins, earrings or any other form of jewelry.

"They seem to be a hot seller," Shannon remarked as two women waited to pay for their souvenirs.

"Yes, people wear their crowns more often than we wear ours," Michel joked.

Every now and then, a stall would have something

unusual, or of finer quality. They happened on one that had some interesting pieces that looked antique. The vendor was an old man who was delighted to show off his wares, or maybe he was just gregarious. He brought out the choicer pieces and told them where he'd acquired them. Although Shannon doubted that a countess would peddle her jewelry to a flea market operator, his stories were fun.

"Do you see anything you like?" Michel asked.

"Everything is lovely, but I really don't need any jewelry."

"Wait!" the man said hastily as they prepared to move on. "I have something very special. I was saving it for a lovely lady like yourself."

He opened a metal strongbox and took out a heart-shaped paperweight made of rose quartz. The lovely, translucent pink stone, slightly smaller than the palm of her hand, was intricately carved all around its perimeter.

"Here, look! Examine!" He held out a magnifying glass.

"Oh, Michel, it's magnificent!" Shannon exclaimed as the glass revealed tiny figures carved in minute detail around the perimeter.

"I knew we'd find something if we looked hard enough." He handed the vendor some bills.

"I don't want you to pay for it."

"It will be my pleasure. A gift gives as much happiness to the donor as to the recipient."

After she had thanked him and they'd walked away, Shannon said, "They save the good stuff for people like you. I'd like to go shopping with you more often."

"That can be arranged." He linked his arm loosely around her shoulders and smiled down at her upturned face.

It was only a companionable gesture, but suddenly the mood changed. His arm tightened and they gazed deeply into each other's eyes.

Funny, Shannon thought, she had envisioned this happening at night, under a black velvet sky. But Michel was just as irresistible in the bright sunshine that highlighted every angle of his aristocratic face.

His mouth was mere inches from hers when a little boy jostled Shannon as he ran after another child. It was a needed wake-up call. Michel released her and they started walking again. His poise was unruffled, and outwardly she managed to give the same impression. But Shannon realized uneasily, that given the right circumstances, things could easily get out of hand between them.

Her slight constraint vanished as they toured the rest of the flea market. They ended up back at the waffle stand, where Michel persuaded Shannon that breakfast was now just a memory. The strawberry-and-whipped-cream-topped waffle was the best she'd ever tasted. Or was it just that everything was better with Michel?

The morning flew by and soon it was time to meet the other couple at the museum.

A guard was posted at the door of the room that housed the crown jewels. That area had been temporarily closed to the public so the four of them could have a private showing.

Marcie and Devon were already there when Shannon and Michel arrived. They were chatting with the curator over coffee. A linen-draped table also held crystal goblets and bottles of wine chilling in a silver tub that looked antique.

Michel introduced Shannon to the curator, Jean Chelfont, a slender gray-haired man who looked like a college professor. They all chatted together for a few moments while a waiter filled thin demitasse cups for the latecomers.

"Wait until you see these jewels," Marcie said to Shannon. "They're to die over!"

"That's an accurate description, unfortunately," Chelfont said. "The Eye of the Leopard, a pear-shaped canary diamond that's the centerpiece of one of our necklaces, was reputedly pried from the altar of an ancient pagan temple. The thief was hunted down and killed, but the diamond wasn't in his possession."

"What did he do with it?" Marcie asked.

"Perhaps he sold or traded it before he was apprehended. The stone disappeared for a long period of time before surfacing in China. History is unclear about how it traveled to Europe, but it was said to have been owned at different times by several members of royalty."

"How did it wind up here?"

Chelfont slanted a glance at Michel before saying, "One of the prince's distant ancestors acquired it."

Michel laughed. "Jean doesn't want to tell you that he probably stole it. Some of the early de Mornays were swashbucklers—if you want to be polite—or brigands if you want to be accurate."

"What fun to have such a colorful background!"

Marcie exclaimed. "I can see you as a pirate, can't you, Shannon?"

"Oh, definitely. He has that devil-may-care wickedness," she teased. "All he needs is a gold hoop earring in one ear."

"And his shirt unbuttoned to the navel," Marcie added. "What do you think?"

"If you're asking me, I think it's time to view the collection," Michel said, smiling.

They were fascinated by the huge Leopard's Eye diamond that dangled from ropes of emeralds and sapphires. Other pieces were equally breathtaking. The two women exclaimed over the precious gems and huge pearls, unable to decide which were their favorites. And then they came to the crowns.

Shannon and Marcie had no trouble deciding which one of these they'd pick. Their unanimous choice was made of filigreed gold covered with pink diamonds, hundreds of them, from "small" one-and-two carat stones to a huge rose-cut center diamond the size of a baby's fist. Woven in among the priceless gems were luminous pearls with a rosy cast. It was as elegant and regal as the other crowns, yet unmistakably feminine.

"Oh, my," Marcie breathed. "Wouldn't you love to have that?"

"Who wouldn't?" Shannon was staring at it, mesmerized. When she realized Michel was watching her, she joked, "Oh well, it probably isn't my size."

"Unfortunately I can't give it to you because it belongs to the monarchy," Michel said. "But you can try it on and see." He lifted the crown from its bed of midnight-blue velvet and placed it on Shannon's head.

They all stared at her for a moment without speaking.

"What?" She looked from one to the other. "Is something wrong?"

"We were thinking how great it looks on you," Marcie said. "You could be a real princess."

"She *is* a real princess," Michel said in a husky voice, raising her hand to his lips.

"For at least another week, anyway," Shannon said, reaching up to remove the jeweled crown. Michel could always be counted on to pay a compliment; she mustn't start believing him.

"The days are going by too fast," Marcie complained.

"You still have all of next week," Devon said. "And don't forget the dinner dance Sunday night."

They made another slow circuit around the room, taking a last look at the crown jewels. After a few moments, Shannon drifted back to watch the curator carefully wrap the pink diamond crown in velvet. Would it stay in its cocoon until Michel married and his wife wore it at occasional state functions? The idea bothered Shannon—solely because such a beautiful thing shouldn't be locked away out of sight, she told herself.

Shannon wore a champagne colored gown to the dinner dance on Sunday night. It had a square portrait neckline and a fitted bodice that flowed into a full skirt with a small train. The television studio must have expected to get a publicity picture of her in the dress, reinforcing the princess theme.

After checking her appearance in a full-length mirror, she joined the others downstairs for a few quiet moments before the guests arrived. Three large reception rooms in one wing of the castle had been opened into each other to form a spacious area. A dance floor, laid over the carpet at one end, had seating for the musicians in back of it.

Small tables and little gold chairs were placed around the perimeter of the room, and the French doors were open to the terrace, where more chairs were scattered about.

"I didn't want to have the party upstairs in the ballroom," Devon explained. "The weather is so nice at this time of year that I thought people might like to stroll in the garden."

"That was a great idea," Marcie said. "We can dance outside too, under the stars."

Michel's attention was focused on Shannon. "How lovely you look." His gaze traveled from the long, shining hair floating around her shoulders, to her tiny waist and the tips of her satin sandals. Belatedly he turned to Marcie. "You look lovely, too."

"Thank you." Her eyes sparkled mischievously as she added, "Now close your eyes."

Michel looked surprised, but he did as she said.

"Okay, tell me what I'm wearing." As he opened his eyes for a quick peek, Marcie laughed. "Don't worry, it's the thought that counts."

Musicians were playing softly when the people started to arrive. Devon had set up an informal receiving line near the door. He explained that it would be easier and faster to introduce the two women as the guests came in, rather than taking them around to each couple or group during the party.

Shannon was positioned between the two men, with Marcie next to Devon on the end. Marcie soon tired of the formalities, however.

"I won't remember any of their names, so why waste good party time?" she whispered to Devon. "I'm going to find some handsome man to dance with."

"I wish I could join you," he said. "Now you know what it's like to stand here endlessly."

"Things could be worse. At least you're not wearing three inch heels." She waggled her fingers and took off.

Everyone was curious about Shannon and inclined to linger in the receiving line, especially the men. They were interested on a personal level, while the women wanted to examine her gown and hairstyle. They could have stood there chatting happily, but Michel was adept at keeping the line moving.

When he and Shannon finally went to mingle with the others, she said, "I promised a lot of men that I'd dance with them, but I don't even know if I'd recognize them again. I met so many people all at once."

"Don't worry about it," Michel said. "They'll come looking for you, I guarantee it. Before they do, may I have this dance?"

"How could I refuse my host, who also happens to be the ruler of the country," she joked.

He took her in his arms and said, "I hoped you would accept because you want to."

"I do," she murmured, tilting her head to look up at him.

Shannon had thought Michel looked sexy in jeans and a T-shirt, but he was positively dazzling in a dinner jacket, black tie and emerald cuff links. She settled into his arms with a sigh of pure pleasure.

They had circled the dance floor only a couple of times when a man approached and asked if he could cut in.

Michel surrendered Shannon with a chuckle. "I didn't expect my prophecy to come true this speedily."

The young man's name was Jonathan. As he danced her away, she said, "I'm rather surprised that protocol allows you to cut in on a prince."

"He's also my host, so he can't very well make a fuss." Jonathan grinned. "Besides, Michel is quite democratic, although I wouldn't want to cross him. The entire council quakes when he's really angry."

"That's hard to imagine. Michel is so...I guess civilized is the word that describes him, or maybe well mannered."

"That's when you know you've gone over the line, when he gets coldly polite. Then you're crossed off the list for good."

"Really?" That didn't describe the man Shannon knew.

Jonathan held her a little closer. "But why are we talking about Michel? I want to know all about *you.*"

This was familiar territory to Shannon—also boring, the same stylized mating dance. She smiled and played the game, because he was a pleasant enough young man. He couldn't help it if he didn't have Michel's bewitching appeal. Few men did.

As soon as their dance was over, other men were waiting to claim Shannon. A man named Terrence, and some others called Mason, Alan and Wesley. She could hardly tell them apart.

When the music finally stopped, she excused herself and went in search of Michel. She found him in a group that included several beautiful women who were hanging on his every word.

He greeted her with a smile and put an arm around her waist. "Are you having a good time?"

"A marvelous time!" Shannon was pleased to see that the women had noticed his embrace. They didn't have to know it was only a casual gesture.

"Michel was telling us the most fascinating story," a gorgeous, green-eyed redhead said. "What happened after the boat tipped over, Michel?"

Shannon never got to hear, because a man came to claim her for the dance she'd evidently promised him.

It was a very glamorous party. Waiters circulated constantly, refilling champagne glasses or taking bar orders. Other waiters passed hot and cold hors d'oeuvres that tasted as good as they looked, although Shannon scarcely had time to eat anything.

Marcie joined her when she was alone for a brief moment. They hadn't seen much of each other until then.

"Isn't it a fabulous party?" Marcie asked.

"Yes, just great," Shannon answered.

Marcie knew her cousin well enough to pick up the slight note of discontent. "Don't tell me you're not having a good time! I saw you dancing every dance with a different guy.''

"That's just it. I've barely seen Michel all night. He danced the first dance with me, that's all. The rest of the time he's been with everybody *but* me.''

"He is one of the hosts, you know. And you're not a wallflower—you're the belle of the ball.''

Shannon smiled wryly. ''I feel like Scarlett O'Hara. I'm afraid I'm going to say fiddle-dee-dee at any minute.''

"There's just no pleasing some people,'' Marcie observed.

Two women joined them, and one of them said to Marcie, ''We've been admiring those marvelous earrings you have on. Would you mind telling us where you bought them?''

"Marcie makes her own jewelry,'' Shannon said, knowing her cousin was a little diffident about her talent. ''Aren't they beautiful?''

"I can't believe it,'' the woman exclaimed. ''I thought surely they was designed by Buccellati, or someone like that.''

"You're very flattering,'' Marcie murmured.

The two women stared at the rough-cut turquoise and lapis stones interspersed with crystal beads that dangled from her ears.

"Would you consider making a pair for me?'' the second woman asked. ''Not an exact copy of yours, of course, although I'd be thrilled to have them. I'll leave the design up to you.''

"Really, it's just a hobby. I don't sell my jewelry.''

"Oh, but you should, my dear!''

They discussed Marcie's work, and tried to get her to change her mind.

When she and Shannon were alone again, Marcie said, "I wonder what they'd say if they knew I made my first piece of jewelry because I couldn't afford to buy the expensive stuff."

"What difference does it make? You have excellent taste and a lot of talent, obviously."

"I know you're prejudiced, but I love you for it," Marcie said fondly.

When she went off to dance, Shannon continued her search for Michel. She found him in a different group this time, but still the center of attention. He welcomed her with a smile, as before, but this time he didn't put his arm around her. Not that it meant anything, Shannon told herself.

Still, she felt like an outsider for the first time. While the others talked animatedly, she gradually edged away.

Shannon wasn't alone for long. A group of young people formed around her. While they were all chatting, the butler announced that a buffet was being served in the dining room.

"Let's take one of those tables on the terrace," Jonathan suggested. "I'll fill a plate for you," he told Shannon. "Save me a seat next to you."

"Well, I..." She looked around for Michel, but couldn't see him.

"Save me the seat on the other side of you," Wesley said.

Their table filled up quickly. Shannon was really miffed at Michel, but her annoyance covered hurt feelings and a sense of disillusionment. She thought

Michel enjoyed her company. Only when his own kind weren't around evidently.

Jonathan returned, juggling plates piled high with seafood and salads and hot dishes, enough food for several people.

"I couldn't begin to eat even a fraction of that," Shannon told him. "But thank you, I know you meant well."

"That's a dangerous assumption to make about Jonathan," said a pretty young woman at the table.

"Don't listen to Chloe, she's my sister," he told Shannon.

"Blame that on our parents," Chloe said with a grin. "They didn't give me a choice."

The conversation was so animated that, at first, nobody noticed Michel standing by their table.

When Jonathan finally became aware of him, he said, "Hey, great party, your highness."

"I'm glad you're enjoying yourself." Michel looked at Shannon impassively. "I came to be sure you had something to eat, but I see you've been well taken care of."

His displeasure was evident and unfair. She'd looked for him repeatedly during the evening. He was the one who hadn't felt the same compulsion! But her grievances weren't as important as healing the rift between them.

"Come and sit with us, Michel," she said. "We can move over and make room. Get another chair, Jonathan."

The young man jumped up immediately, but Michel held out his hand. "Don't bother. I want to check on the other guests."

As soon as she could leave gracefully, Shannon excused herself. She found Michel having a drink with some of the couples who were in no hurry to go to the buffet table.

Shannon didn't bother to make small talk. She got right to the point. "May I speak to you for a moment, Michel, alone?"

"Of course." He led her a few steps away, to the middle of the room.

She knew it would be only a matter of minutes until other guests would join them, so she said, "Can we go someplace more private?"

"If I didn't know better, I'd think you were being provocative. What's the matter, are you tired of all your young men?" When she looked at him mutely, Michel said, "We can walk in the garden if you like."

Neither of them said anything until they had followed the path to a secluded spot, out of sight of the party.

Then Shannon said, "I'm not sure what you're angry at me about, but I'd like to clear the air between us."

"What makes you think I'm angry?"

"Oh, please, Michel! You haven't come near me all evening."

"Are you claiming you were neglected? You looked as if you were having a good time."

"I was, I mean, I am. It's a wonderful party."

"Then I'm afraid I don't understand your complaint."

"I'd like to have spent a little time with you."

"I was in plain sight all evening. You could have joined me at any time."

"I *did,* a couple of times. But you barely noticed. Your admiring subjects were more engrossing," she couldn't help adding.

"What would you have me do, ignore them? I *am* the host this evening—at least, one of them."

Shannon had thought they could talk things out, but Michel didn't care to. She wasn't that important to him. She turned away. "Well, I won't keep you from your guests any longer."

"Shannon, wait!" He caught her hand. "I'm sorry. I've been acting like an insecure teenager. I apologize."

"I don't want an apology. I want to know what I did wrong? You didn't seem to mind that I was dancing with your friends. I thought that was what you wanted."

"It would have been nice if we could have had supper together," he answered indirectly.

"I asked you to join us. Jonathan would have gotten you a chair."

Michel's face hardened. "Was I supposed to displace someone because of my rank? Or perhaps you expected me to hover in the background with a plate on my knee."

Was his dignity affronted, or did he really feel slighted? It was a shock to discover that a ruling prince could have as fragile an ego as other men. Another possibility was that he actually cared about her. The idea that Michel might be jealous made Shannon almost giddy with happiness.

"You're absolutely right, Michel," she said demurely. "It was thoughtless of me not to wait and see if you intended to ask me to sit with you. I just got the impression that you preferred to be with your friends."

"That would certainly include you."

"You know what I mean."

His autocratic expression was replaced by amusement. "A man is no match for a manipulative woman. In a moment I'll be apologizing for ignoring you all night, when we both know it was the other way around."

"It wasn't by choice," she said softly. "We both thought we were acting terribly civilized, which can make for misunderstandings. People should come right out and say what they want."

Michel chuckled. "Men have gotten their faces slapped for doing that."

"I'm just glad all is forgiven. It is, isn't it?"

"I'm fine with it if you are." His eyes gleamed in the starlight as he moved closer to her. "Pacts are usually sealed in some fashion."

"What did you have in mind?" Shannon knew exactly. She lifted her face to his, feeling excitement race through her veins like wildfire. She had wondered what Michel's firm mouth would feel like, moving over hers. Now she was about to find out.

He clasped her slender waist and drew her slowly toward him. His head lowered to hers, blotting out everything but her awareness of him, the strength yet gentleness of his hands at her waist, the total masculinity of the man. Her lips parted softly.

Then they heard laughter and voices coming down the path. Michel's hands tightened for an instant and he uttered a sound of annoyance. Then he released her. By the time the guests reached them, they were starting back to the party.

"I suppose I'll have to settle for holding you in my arms on the dance floor," he remarked wryly.

Shannon hid her disappointment under a light tone. "Don't count on it. Someone will cut in."

"Not this time. I've been a good host long enough."

The radiant stars in the sky were reflected in her eyes as they walked along the path, hand in hand.

Chapter Eight

The party lasted until the early hours of the morning, but Shannon didn't want it to end. After she and Michel had made up, it was a fairy-tale evening.

They danced together, and he kept his promise. When someone asked to cut in, Michel simply said no. It didn't take long until his meaning became clear.

At first, Shannon worried that people would get the wrong idea about them. Then she decided, so what if they thought she and Michel were having an affair? It wouldn't be his first, and none of her friends or family would hear about it. Not that there was anything to hear. She couldn't help feeling a small pang of regret, but that was better than having something to be *really* sorry about.

When the party was finally over, Devon suggested having a nightcap to unwind and compare notes on the evening.

"I've barely seen you and Shannon all night," he said to his brother.

Michel took off his tie and unfastened the top buttons of his dress shirt. "You three can stay up and discuss the party. I'm going to bed. I'll meet you all for a late breakfast tomorrow."

"I've had it, too," Shannon said. "I think I've worn my three-inch heels down to two inches."

"Devon and I are wide-awake," Marcie complained.

"Then party on with our blessings," Michel said. "I'm going to check the fax machine in my office, and then I'm through for the night."

Shannon went upstairs without waiting for him and began to get undressed. She hung her lovely gown on a padded hanger in the dressing room, before putting on her nightgown. The maid would have done it in the morning, but as Shannon had laughingly told Marcie, she didn't want to get accustomed to a lifestyle she could never afford.

Although it was very late and she was pleasantly tired, Shannon wanted to savor all the high points of the evening one more time. She drifted over to the French doors and went out onto the balcony in her bare feet.

Gazing up at the moon, she thought about Michel and how different their lives might be if she were a real princess. Tonight could have been their engagement party. The wedding would be a lot more elaborate of course, dictated by strict rules of protocol, but they would be able to plan their own honeymoon. The fantasy was rapidly becoming real as Shannon let her imagination soar.

Michel might want to go on a private yacht, just the two of them, making love all night and calling at glamorous ports during the day. Shannon didn't really care where they went, she would be content to stay right here in the castle. Would he move into her apartment, or would she move into his? They'd have to discuss that.

A slight sound made her turn. It didn't surprise her to see Michel standing in the shadows at the other end of the terrace. They were so attuned to each other that he always knew when she wanted him. She began to walk slowly in his direction.

Michel had come outside when he found that he was too restless to sleep. He couldn't get the misunderstanding with Shannon out of his mind. He'd behaved badly, which was totally unlike him. But what bothered him was the reason he was so curt with her. He had been jealous when she seemed to welcome the attention of other men, forgetting about *him* completely.

Michel couldn't recall ever being jealous before. He'd simply never cared that much. Why did it bother him to see Shannon enjoying herself in another man's arms? It wasn't as if he was in love with her. She was beautiful and charming, and he wanted very much to make love to her, but nothing more. He certainly didn't want to get involved.

His introspection was interrupted when Shannon came outside unexpectedly, almost as though he'd summoned her. A strong tide of desire surged through him as he stared at the perfection of her nearly nude body, clearly visible in the moonlight. The diaphanous gown veiled her nakedness provocatively without hiding anything from his avid gaze. Michel drew in his breath sharply when she started toward him.

Shannon was hypnotized by her own fantasy. She smiled dreamily as she went to meet her perfect groom, but when Michel took her in his arms, she was jolted back to reality. His hard, lithe body wasn't part of a dream!

"My beautiful, golden-haired angel," he murmured, sliding his lips over her bare shoulder.

She stiffened in his arms. "I didn't know you were out here," she gasped.

He smiled fondly. "Don't be shy with me, darling."

"It isn't that...I mean, I was just..."

Shannon felt disoriented and Michel was adding to her confusion. His hands were caressing her back while he dropped tiny kisses behind her ear, on her eyelids, at the corner of her mouth. She turned her head restlessly.

"I've wanted to hold you like this since the first moment I saw you," he said in a husky voice. "I didn't think it would happen this way."

"It wasn't supposed to! You don't understand."

"It's all right, sweetheart," he said soothingly. "We don't have to play games with each other."

Shannon had to tell him what happened. But how could she explain that she'd stepped through the looking glass into a romantic world that had seemed real? It was difficult enough without his mouth distracting her and his hands making her heart race.

"Please, Michel," she said faintly.

"Yes, darling. Tell me what you want." He urged

her hips closer to his. "I want to make you so happy."

"You do," she sighed as their breath mingled and she stopped trying to explain the inexplicable.

His mouth closed over hers with a low, masculine sound of pleasure. Shannon put her arms around his neck and her body seemed to melt into his. They were joined in almost every way possible. His deep, penetrating kiss was everything she'd dreamed it would be.

But when Michel stroked her breast, circling her nipple erotically, she drew in her breath sharply and her body tensed. She knew vaguely that now was the time to stop. He was sliding the straps of her gown off her shoulders.

"We shouldn't be doing this." She tried to sound forceful, but her voice was a plaintive murmur.

"It's all right. No one can see us up here."

"That's not what I..." Her protest died as her gown slithered to the tile floor and he reached for her.

"You're so exquisite." His eyes gleamed in the moonlight as he gazed at her nude body.

He feathered his fingertips over her shoulders, her breasts. When he stroked her loins, Shannon trembled with a passion she'd never experienced.

"You're cold, darling," Michel said, misinterpreting. He lifted her in his arms. "I'll take you inside."

She trembled even more, but with anticipation. Nothing mattered but lying in his arms and having him fill her with joy.

"I've never wanted any woman the way I want you," he said in a throaty voice. "We're going to be so good together."

The words hit a discordant note, puncturing her rosy bubble and letting in the cold air of reason. Other men had used those same words when they were trying to coax her to have sex. That's what she would be doing with Michel—having sex, not making love. She struggled out of his arms and reached down for her nightgown.

He stared at her in bewilderment. "What's wrong, Shannon? What just happened?"

"It's late. I have to go to my room," she mumbled.

Michel caught her shoulder as she turned away, clutching her nightgown to hide her nakedness. "You can't walk away without telling me why," he said. "Did I do something to offend you?"

"No, it wasn't that."

"Then what? You wanted me as much as I want you. I'm not mistaken about that."

She wasn't a good enough actress to deny it. He was too knowledgeable about women to believe her, anyway. "I just...changed my mind, that's all. Please let me go, Michel."

"Of course." He released her immediately.

Shannon stole a quick glance at his face. His expression was austere in the moonlight. He must think she was what all men held in contempt—a tease. And she couldn't even explain. She turned and ran swiftly back to her room.

Shannon had never been more miserable in her life, but she knew she'd done the right thing. She could so easily fall in love with Michel, but they had no future together. He would break her heart.

Shannon didn't fall asleep until dawn was breaking, and then she only slept fitfully. It was an effort to drag herself out of bed. She dreaded going down to breakfast and facing Michel. What would she say to him? Even worse, what would he say to her?

She showered and dressed in jeans and a red sweatshirt. It didn't matter what she looked like. Michel wouldn't notice or care. Maybe he wouldn't show up this morning. He could always make the excuse that he had royal business to attend to. The thought cheered her somewhat.

But when Shannon went down to the small dining room where they usually gathered for breakfast, Michel was sitting at the table with Marcie and his brother. Both men stood politely when she entered the room. Shannon said a general "Good morning," then slipped quickly into a chair.

"I was just about to come up and roust you out of bed," Marcie said. "It's not like you to sleep this late. You went up earlier than I did."

A servant answered the bell Michel rang, and asked what Shannon wanted for breakfast.

After she had given her order, Marcie said, "Is that all you're going to have, juice and coffee? You should try the blueberry crepes. They're fabulous with the country ham."

"How can you eat again after that huge buffet last night?"

"That was yesterday. Today comes with a whole new set of meals."

"By the time we leave, they'll charge you for two seats on the airplane," Shannon warned.

"Don't talk about going home. I've decided to stay here."

"And do what?" Shannon asked.

"Well, let's see. Maybe I could be a party planner," Marcie joked. "You'll give me a reference, won't you, Devon?"

"Absolutely! We'll have to find something for Shannon, too. What would you suggest, Michel?"

"She's good at games," he said, gazing at her without expression. "Perhaps something in that field."

"That's a great idea." Marcie hadn't picked up on their tension. "Shannon is wonderful with children."

She managed a slight laugh. "You're making our hosts nervous. Don't worry," she told Michel, gazing at him with the same directness he'd leveled at her. "You might have to evict Marcie, but I'll be gone soon."

Devon gave them a puzzled look and glanced at Marcie for enlightenment. She shrugged slightly, indicating she didn't know, either.

"Well, let's talk about tonight," Devon said. "What does everybody feel like doing?"

Michel and Shannon both answered at once. He said he had a previous engagement; she said she was going to bed early.

"Then I guess Marcie and I are on our own." Devon looked at the other two covertly for a moment. "But we'll expect you to join us for croquet this afternoon. I promised I'd teach Marcie to play, and we need four people for a real match."

"As a matter of fact, I—" Michel began.

Devon cut in deftly. "I'm sure you can spare an hour or two. If you try to get out of it, I'll want a detailed explanation of what you plan to do that's more important,'' he said in a playful voice. ''You, too, Shannon.''

Neither wanted to make an issue of it, so they reluctantly agreed. Marcie tried to get her cousin alone to find out what was wrong, but Shannon eluded her and went for a solitary walk.

They all assembled on the lawn at the appointed time, some with more enthusiasm than others. Wickets were spaced in a pattern over the lush grass, and the croquet equipment was stacked neatly in a stand.

''This won't be any fun for you, Devon,'' Shannon protested. ''Marcie and I don't know how to play.''

''We'll teach you,'' he said.

Standing in front of them, he demonstrated how to hit the ball through the wicket with the mallet, or to knock an opponent's ball away. It looked childishly simple, until they tried it—over and over again.

''Why won't the darn ball go where I want it to?'' Shannon exclaimed in frustration after she knocked the ball five feet past the wicket, then farther than that on the return shot. ''It isn't as if I'm uncoordinated. I play tennis year-round in California.''

Michel laughed at her exasperated expression. The tension between them had gradually dissipated once they began to play. The exercise and concentration on the game served to distract them from their personal problems.

''You'll get the hang of it with a little practice,'' he said. ''Here, let me show you. You have to square up your mallet.''

He made the necessary adjustment. Shannon hit the

ball with the same result, only this time the ball flew off at an angle.

"I did just what you said, and look what happened," she complained. "I'm getting worse instead of better."

"You turned your mallet again. Try it this way." He moved in back of her and put his arms around her, grasping her forearms. "Take the mallet straight back, like a golf club, then you'll hit the ball square. See? Just like a pro."

Shannon watched the ball travel straight toward the wicket. "But I didn't really do that. You had your hands on my arms." She turned her head to look up at him.

Neither of them realized until then that he hadn't released her—or even that he'd put his arms around her. The physical contact between them revived their awareness of each other, although both tried to hide it.

As the game progressed, however, everything was smoothed over again. Shannon had finally "gotten the hang of it," as Michel promised, so it turned into a spirited game.

Devon had prudently taken her as his partner, after the inexplicable coolness she and his brother had showed toward each other at breakfast. Michel and Marcie were their opponents. At one point, Shannon had an opportunity to knock Michel's ball away, but she missed the shot. Marcie cheered and Devon groaned.

A few moments later, when they were waiting for their turn, Michel said to Shannon, "You couldn't have missed me from that distance. Why didn't you knock my ball away?''

She gave him a wide-eyed look. "I'm just a beginner. I'm doing the best I can."

"That's just the point, you weren't, and I want to know why."

"I guess I don't have the killer instinct." When he simply looked at her, waiting for the real reason, Shannon glanced away and said, "Okay, maybe I thought I owed it to you."

"For last night? That would scarcely suffice," he said dryly.

"It's the best I can do."

"No, you can do one more thing. You can tell me why you changed your mind so suddenly."

"I wasn't playing games, as you seem to think."

"I'm sorry for that. It was a boorish thing to say."

"Yes, well, it would be nice if we could forget about it and be friends again. It was something that just happened."

Before Michel could answer, Marcie called from the other end of the grass court, "Hey, you guys, have you forgotten we're playing a game here?"

Shannon was afraid Michel would become cool and distant again. She hadn't given him an answer, so his ego was still bruised. But to her relief, he was still his old self—well, almost. A little of the warmth was missing, and all of the magnetic attraction, at least for him. Michel wasn't interested in her anymore. That was a good thing, Shannon told herself. It was a lot more important to maintain a friendly relationship.

She couldn't fault his behavior the rest of the afternoon. They played several hard-fought games, then relaxed on the terrace drinking lemonade and swapping stories about the games they'd played when they were children.

"I always thought croquet was a children's game," Marcie remarked.

"Not at all," Devon said. "It started in France in the seventeen hundreds and was very popular in Victorian England. It's been around for a long time. There are a lot of exclusive croquet clubs in your own country."

"They'd have to be exclusive to maintain a grass court like yours," Marcie joked. "Everybody at home describes their gardeners in three words—mow, blow, go."

When they were all relaxed and mellow and Devon thought the mild tiff—or whatever it was—had passed, he said casually, "Would you two like to change your minds about tonight? Marcie and I are just going to do something casual."

Michel answered before Shannon. "I wish I could, but as I said, I have an engagement. Actually I'd forgotten about it, but Olivia reminded me last night at the party."

Olivia could be a silver-haired dowager, but Shannon very much doubted it. She believed that Michel had a date, but not a long-standing one. You could always tell when someone was telling a lie. They went into needless detail.

"Shannon?" Devon was looking at her questioningly. "How about you? Will you join us?"

"Yes, I'd like to." There was no reason for her to stay home. Michel wasn't going to. "I feel a lot more rested than I did this morning,'' she added, remembering the excuse she'd given.

Devon took them to a wonderful restaurant for dinner, where they got the royal treatment even without Michel. Of course Devon was a prince, too, Shannon reminded herself. Why couldn't she have been attracted to him? He was so much more uncomplicated than his brother.

After dinner they went to a popular musical. Marcie had read about it in the entertainment section of the local newspaper. Their seats were in a box near the stage.

It was a wonderful evening, and Shannon enjoyed herself. But she thought about Michel frequently, wondering if he was at a festive party with a lot of glamorous guests. Or was it a smaller, more intimate party for just two people?

Shannon refused to let it spoil her evening. Michel might have made this date when he was annoyed with her. He couldn't very well break it at the last minute. Tomorrow everything would be fine.

It didn't start out that way. Michel wasn't at breakfast.

"We won't wait for him," Devon said. "He might be working."

"I wouldn't be surprised. We haven't given him much time to run the country," Marcie commented.

"He'll probably join us later. Would you ladies like to go to the races today?"

After breakfast, Devon tracked his brother down. He found him in his office, as he'd surmised. "You missed a smashing show last night," he said. "It deserved all the rave notices it received."

"I'm glad you enjoyed yourself."

"Did you have a good evening?"

"Very nice." Michel shuffled some papers on his desk, but Devon didn't take the hint.

"We missed you at breakfast this morning."

"I had coffee sent up to my apartment." Michel rather pointedly picked up an official-looking document.

"I'm taking the ladies to the races this afternoon," Devon said. "You're welcome to join us."

"I can't. I have work to do."

"Do you think the people would revolt if you took another afternoon off?" Devon asked, in what he thought was a humorous tone.

Michel abruptly lost his temper. "If you had any idea of the duties this job entails, you wouldn't find it such a laughing matter. I've tried to get you to take a more active part, but you refuse to assume any of the responsibilities."

"That's not fair, Michel! I may think a lot of the pomp and ceremony is unnecessary, but I do whatever you ask me to."

"With a singular lack of enthusiasm."

"Because we both know it's just busywork. Any important decisions have to be made by you. That's not what this is about. I'm sorry if something has upset you, but is it fair to take it out on me?"

Michel ran his fingers through his thick hair. "No, you're right. I've had a lot on my mind lately and it's made me short-tempered. I apologize."

"That's not necessary." Devon hesitated for a moment. "Would you like to talk about whatever is bothering you?"

"Thanks, but I'm used to handling problems."

"I'm aware of that. But sometimes when a couple has had a misunderstanding, it helps to discuss it with a sympathetic third party."

Michel's expression turned austere. "What makes you think my problem is personal?"

"I don't know. I just assumed—"

"Assumptions are unreliable. Now if you'll excuse me, I have a lot of work to do." Michel's tone precluded any further attempt at discussion.

Devon didn't tell the others ahead of time that Michel wouldn't be joining them that afternoon. Marcie found out before Shannon because she came downstairs first.

"That's too bad," she said. "Did something important come up?"

"Yes. Michel has a meeting with some foreign dignitary. He arrived unexpectedly."

Marcie gave him a penetrating look. "What's really going on, Devon? Why isn't your brother coming with us today?"

"I think it has something to do with Shannon. You must have noticed that they were acting strangely toward each other at breakfast yesterday."

"Yes, they did seem kind of cranky, both of them. I was going to ask her about it, but she just sort of disappeared." Marcie looked thoughtful. "That wasn't like her. But they seemed perfectly normal while we were playing croquet, so I forgot about it."

"I thought everything was fine, too, but now I can't

help wondering. Oh, well, I'm sure whatever it is will blow over.''

Shannon hid her disappointment when she found out Michel wasn't going to the races with them. She was aware that the other two were watching her closely. Was it that obvious Michel lit up her life? She'd have to get better at hiding her emotions.

Michel watched them leave from his office window, his gaze lingering on Shannon. In her white linen suit and a blue-and-white striped silk blouse, she looked cool and sophisticated—and achingly desirable.

His decision not to join them today had been the correct one, Michel told himself. The attraction he felt toward Shannon would bring nothing but trouble. She wasn't the sort of woman you had a brief fling with and then remembered fondly. She could torment a man with memories if he were foolish enough to get involved.

The practical solution was to stay away from her, but it left him dissatisfied. He'd never met a woman he wanted this much. Not just physically, although he ached to hold her in his arms and bring her more pleasure than she'd ever known. But he also admired her quick mind and her sunny disposition. And then there was her complete lack of guile, so rare in the women he knew. He couldn't think of one thing about her that he'd change. So why couldn't he simply enjoy whatever time they had together?

Shannon was attracted to him, too. The chemistry between them might very well ignite, which was another reason to stay away from her. She was living in a fairy-tale world, where a relationship with a prince meant living happily ever after. Unfortunately life wasn't that idyllic. There would be personal sacrifices involved that she might bitterly regret, and he didn't want to be responsible for making her unhappy.

Michel thrust his hands deep into his pockets and paced the floor. He was doing the right thing in keeping his distance. Shannon would be gone soon, and neither of them would have anything to regret. His eyes were bleak as he admitted that wasn't true for him.

Devon and the two women had a late lunch in the clubhouse, where they met a lot of the guests from his party. A steady stream of them sat at their table for a while, then were replaced with others. They all reiterated what a great time they'd had and chatted casually. It gave Shannon and Marcie a nice sense of belonging.

Everybody asked where Michel was, and didn't seem overly surprised to find out he was working. So maybe it was true, Shannon thought, feeling suddenly better.

As one couple left to go down to the paddock, the woman, said, "We'll see all of you at our place Wednesday night."

"It sounds delightful, Caroline, but am I supposed to know about it?" Devon asked.

"Don't tell me Michel didn't mention it? That man! I knew I should have called you, Devon. We're having a little gathering. A casual evening for just good friends. Do say you can come."

After looking inquiringly at Shannon and Marcie, he said, "We'd be happy to."

"Splendid! And tell Michel I'm expecting him, too."

When the three of them were alone briefly, Devon said, "I hope you like parties, because everyone wants to entertain for you."

"Her party is for us? Wow!" Marcie exclaimed. "We're celebrities, Shannon."

"I wonder why Michel didn't mention it," she said slowly.

"It probably slipped his mind. You should see how loaded his desk is." Devon dismissed the subject. "Have you both decided what horse you like in the next race?"

It was an enjoyable afternoon, like everything he planned. By the time they were driven back to the castle, Shannon was convinced that she'd been paranoid for thinking Michel was avoiding her.

They were relaxing on the terrace, having tall cool drinks and discussing plans for the evening, when Michel joined them.

"Am I looking at a bunch of happy winners?" he asked with a smile.

"Devon won, but Shannon and I didn't," Marcie said. "Why is it the rich get richer?"

"Not always," Devon said. "This was just one of my good days."

"He has bad ones, I can assure you," Michel said, sitting on the foot of Shannon's chaise.

They discussed racing and the friends they'd run into at the track. "Caroline was miffed that you didn't tell us about her party on Wednesday," Devon said.

"Her 'casual' evening? That means a minimum of fifty people."

"We still have to go."

"I don't think I'll ever get so jaded that I won't want to go to a party," Marcie observed.

"You and Devon make a good pair," Michel said. "I can't keep up with him."

Devon raised an eyebrow. "Do you expect anybody to believe that? Your social life has been rather widely documented."

"Then why go into it now?" Michel asked lightly.

Devon took the hint. "We were discussing what we feel like doing tonight. Any suggestions?"

"I'm sure you'll think of something. Unfortunately I won't be able to join you," Michel said without explanation. "Well, back to work." He rose. "I haven't finished reading the global economy reports."

After he left, even Marcie didn't speculate on the reason Michel was bowing out again. Devon suggested things they could do, but Shannon made excuses.

"You and Marcie go without me," she said. "Michel was right about you two. I can't keep up with you, either."

They tried to coax her, but she remained firm. A short time later, she went up to her suite where she spent a quiet evening reading—or at least trying to. She usually enjoyed a night alone with a good book although they weren't too frequent, even at home. But that night she felt restless.

Finally she gave up and went outside on the terrace. It was balmy out, as it had been the fateful night that had ruined everything between herself and Michel.

Still Shannon couldn't regret those stirring few minutes in his arms when she'd learned the passion she was capable of. The memory of his hands caressing her nude body, his mouth teasing her erotically, made her shiver with remembered pleasure.

She glanced down the terrace at Michel's darkened windows. Who was he out with this evening? The same woman as last night, or a different one? Shannon had no doubt that he was with a woman. He had spent an entire, platonic week with herself and Marcie. It was too much to ask such a virile man to remain celibate any longer than that.

Was this the way it was going to be for the rest of her stay? It was time to put him in the finished-business file.

Chapter Nine

Michel had taken off his tie and was unbuttoning his shirt when there was a knock on the door. "I should have put out a Do Not Disturb sign like they do in hotels," he muttered, striding to the door.

Devon was standing in the hall. "You're home early," he observed.

"Did you make a special trip to tell me that?" Michel drawled.

"I don't know where you were tonight, but it's obvious that you had a rotten time. You could have stayed here and done that."

Michel glanced down the hall toward Shannon's rooms, then motioned his brother inside. "I'm sorry for being curt, but I'm tired and I'd like to go to bed. Unless this is something urgent, I'd prefer to discuss it in the morning."

"I'll try to be brief. I want to talk to you about Shannon."

"I'll make it easy for you. The conversation is over."

"Don't pull rank on me, Michel. I'm not seeking an audience with my liege. This is just brother to brother."

"My answer is the same." Michel's generous mouth thinned.

"All right, we won't discuss her. You can simply listen to what I have to say. I don't know what went on between you two, but—"

Michel cut him off. "Your curiosity is distasteful— brother or no brother. And although it's none of your business, nothing went on, as you so euphemistically put it."

"If you expect anyone to believe that, you'd better take acting lessons. It's obvious that you two have had some kind of disagreement. We were all having a great time together, and then something went wrong. All I know is that it happened the night of the party."

Michel had made a conscious effort not to think about that night, the scent of Shannon's perfume in his nostrils, the satin smoothness of her bare skin as his hands glided over her body. He didn't welcome the reminder.

"I'm not suggesting it was your fault," Devon continued as his brother walked over to a bar cart and poured a drink for each of them. "People can say something perfectly innocent, and it's taken out of context by the other person."

Michel was caught between amusement and annoyance. "You mean, if I propositioned her, you're sure it wasn't done crudely."

"That possibility never entered my mind," Devon protested. "You're too much of a gentleman to ever be guilty of that kind of conduct. I just want to find out why you're avoiding Shannon. You seemed to enjoy her company. Then suddenly, just like that, you became unavailable."

"I think I've fulfilled any obligations I had as a host, considering that I didn't invite any of them here in the first place. Do you recall telling me that I'd hardly know they were around? That you'd take full responsibility for entertaining them."

"And I was prepared to. You were the one who decided to join in the things I planned—after you met Shannon. Anyone could see there was an attraction between you two. If the novelty has worn off and you've grown tired of her, you could have made it a little less obvious. You don't spend every day and night with a person, and then stop seeing them entirely."

Michel drained his drink and poured himself another. "I'm sure she couldn't care less."

"You're wrong. I can tell she's hurt. She wouldn't even come with Marcie and me tonight. Shannon stayed home alone."

"Did it ever occur to you that not everyone likes to party every night? Maybe she was simply tired."

Devon sighed. "All right, Michel. If you don't want to talk about it, I can't make you. I just thought I could persuade you to suffer through a little more of Shannon's company."

"You know I didn't consider it a hardship. Shannon is a lovely, charming woman. She's just not for me.''

"Nobody is asking you to become emotionally involved. If she were going to be here longer, perhaps something might have developed. The world is changing. It isn't unheard-of for a royal to marry a commoner these days.''

"That doesn't concern me,'' Michel said. "I'm not interested in getting married. You're the one who should be thinking of settling down.''

"You're just trying to change the subject. There's no pressure on me to get married. You're the one responsible for producing an heir to the throne, not I.''

"You never know what's in the cards. That's why I keep trying to get you to develop leadership qualities. So you can take over someday—if necessary.''

Devon looked at his brother in concern. "Is there something you're not telling me? I've had the feeling lately that something is troubling you. Are you ill? Is it serious? Whatever it is, we'll get the best doctors and they'll know what to do.''

Michel's taut body relaxed and he put a hand on his brother's shoulder. "I didn't mean to scare you. There's nothing wrong with my health. Look at me. Do I look sick?''

Devon gazed earnestly at him. If ever there was a man in his prime, it was Michel. His body was lean and muscular, his strong face was unlined. Yet he was clearly under stress.

"I'm sorry if I've been short-tempered lately,'' Michel said. "Sometimes things pile up, and I get frustrated like anyone else.''

"I guess I should take more interest in affairs of state," Devon said in a muted voice. "Then maybe I could share the burden."

"That would be nice," Michel said dryly.

"I'm going to change—at least, I'll try."

Michel returned his brother's tentative smile. "I'll try, also. I didn't realize I was neglecting our guests. I can't promise to spend as much time with them as I did before, but I'll definitely join you on occasion."

Devon left feeling he'd accomplished his mission, and Michel's spirits were lighter than they had been. Devon clearly had a point. It was unkind, as well as bad manners, to suddenly ignore Shannon.

She might even think he'd lost interest because she'd changed her mind about making love, which was always a woman's privilege. He certainly wouldn't want her to think he was sulking like a frustrated schoolboy!

It was the right decision to keep an emotional distance from Shannon, but he could still enjoy her company now and then. That was the mature way to handle the matter.

Michel unfastened his gold cuff links and removed his shirt, already looking forward with anticipation to the next morning. Where should he take them that they hadn't been already? Someplace special, he decided as he tossed aside the rest of his clothes and got into bed.

Michel was already sitting at the table reading the morning newspaper when the other three came down to breakfast.

"Hi, stranger," Marcie said. "Long time, no see."

Shannon wouldn't have mentioned his recent absence, but her cousin saw no reason not to. She really had the right idea—say what's on your mind. It cleared the air for all of them.

"It's only been a couple of days," Michel said with a smile. "I had to take time off to enact some new laws."

"Then you're excused," Marcie said. "We missed you, though."

"That's the story of my life." Devon heaved a mock sigh. "Big brother is always the star, and I'm just second banana."

"You know that's not so," Shannon said. Even though she knew he was joking, this was a good chance to express their appreciation. "We've had a wonderful time with you."

"He knows it," Michel said. "That's my brother's devious way of getting compliments."

"You don't have to tell all our family secrets," Devon said.

They were joking together unselfconsciously, as though there had been no glitch in their relationship. The initial tension Shannon had felt was gone.

"Now that I'm back in vacation mode, I have a suggestion for today," Michel said. "We've covered most of the urban sights, so I thought you might like to take a picnic lunch to our country lodge and spend the day. It's a nice drive from here. We often spent family vacations there, hiking and fishing."

"It sounds great!" Shannon said. "I used to go fishing with my father."

"That's one yes vote. Do you two want to make it unanimous?" Michel looked at the other couple.

Devon exchanged a glance with Marcie. "Well, the thing is, today is the annual dog show. It's a big deal, and a lot of our friends show their dogs," Devon explained to Shannon.

"We ran into some people named Wainwright last night at one of the clubs," Marcie said. "Friends of Devon's. They breed Irish Wolfhounds. They're showing one of them today, and then they're going to have a big get-together afterward, hopefully a blue-ribbon celebration."

"You and Shannon are invited, of course," Devon told his brother.

Michel looked at Shannon, who said tepidly, "Well, if that's what everybody wants to do."

"It's going to be fabulous!" Marcie said. "Devon says they have private boxes to watch the judging, and everybody gets all dressed up. Just like Ascot in England."

"Scarcely." Devon laughed. "About the only similarity is that all the animals involved have four legs."

"It's very posh, anyway."

Michel was looking at Shannon. "That's not really what you feel like doing, is it?"

"Don't be a party pooper, Shannon," Marcie pleaded.

"We're not joined at the hip," Devon said. "If Marcie wants to go to the dog show, and Shannon wants to spend the day in the country, why don't we go our separate ways and meet back here for dinner?"

"Sounds sensible to me," Michel said. "Wear jeans and comfortable shoes," he told Shannon. "I'll tell Jennings to have a picnic basket prepared for us."

At first she was glad the matter had been settled to

everybody's satisfaction. But Shannon suddenly realized that she and Michel would be alone together, without the other couple for a buffer.

Then she told herself it didn't matter. She and Michel had gotten past their little misunderstanding. There wouldn't be any awkward moments. They'd both learned from experience.

The road to the lodge led through lush countryside that Shannon hadn't seen before. The drive took about an hour, but it sped by as Michel told her about the days when his ancestors had made the trip by horseback. The surrounding countryside was filled with wild animals then, some of them dangerous, like wolves and bears.

"They're long gone, of course. Now, the only wolves wear dinner jackets and prefer to eat caviar rather than people," Michel joked.

"Wolves in formal clothing can be just as dangerous," Shannon remarked lightly.

"Not necessarily. All you have to do is rap them smartly on the snout and they go off in search of easier prey."

She didn't even have to do that to discourage *him,* Shannon thought ironically, then put the memory out of her mind.

The tall iron fence surrounding the grounds of the lodge was camouflaged by dense foliage and vines. Massive iron gates marked the entrance, the only indication of man's incursion into nature.

Michel pushed an electronic opener and the gates slid apart silently, then closed after they had driven through. There was nobody in the gatehouse, or working on the grounds on either side of the long driveway that cut through woods and meadowlands.

"Doesn't anybody live here?" Shannon asked.

"Not at the present time. Our caretaker retired recently, and I haven't replaced him yet."

"Don't you have a staff to take care of the house and grounds? It seems so deserted here. At the castle there are servants everywhere."

"I have a staff that comes in every morning to clean, and a crew that takes care of the grounds. They're local people who live around here. There's no reason for them to stay after they've finished their work."

"You're a great boss. Most people want their workers to put in a set amount of hours."

Michel shrugged. "What matters is how well they do the job, not how long it takes them. I've had no cause for complaint."

The lodge appeared suddenly around a bend in the road. The two-story stone building looked ancient and austere, more a man's retreat than a woman's.

"I can see why you like it here," Shannon commented as Michel stopped the car by the studded and barred front door. "It looks like you."

"Ancient?" He grinned as he got out and walked around to her side.

"No, slightly forbidding, though."

Michel extended his hand to help her out of the car. "Don't pretend you're awed by me. You've been leading me on a merry chase ever since you got here."

He was smiling, but Shannon knew they were getting into dangerous waters. "Well, fortunately for you, I won't be here much longer," she said in a light tone. "Don't forget the picnic basket is in the trunk."

"I'm glad you reminded me." He opened the front door with a large, hand-forged key. "You can go in and look around while I retrieve our lunch."

The inside of the lodge had a much warmer feeling than the outside. The sizable living room was furnished casually, unlike the castle with its priceless antiques. Comfortable couches and chairs were grouped around the room, and fleecy rugs covered areas of the stone floors.

Michel joined her as she was gazing around. "Well, what do you think of the place? Does it still look like me?"

"Only when you're in one of your informal moods," she teased. "I want to see the rest of it."

After they had toured the house, which was spacious yet relatively unpretentious, Michel said, "It's a little early for lunch. Would you like to go fishing, or just take a walk in the woods?"

"Let's go fishing. We can hike afterward. Is there a lake here somewhere? I didn't see one."

"There's a stream at the bottom of that little hill over there that runs all through the property. It's stocked with trout."

"That's what my dad and I used to fish for. Betcha a quarter I catch more fish than you do."

"That's not much of a bet."

"I'm not much of a gambler," Shannon laughed. "Why don't we decide on the prize after one of us wins?"

"You're taking a chance, considering I'm going to beat you."

Michel gave her a melting smile. "Not nearly as big a chance as you're taking."

"You know what they say about being overconfident," she warned.

"No, what do they say?"

"I don't know, either, but there's a saying for everything."

They bantered back and forth, all the way across the lawn and down to the water, a charming little stream that burbled over submerged rocks.

A small shed housed every conceivable kind of fishing gear, rods and reels, nets, wading boots and so on. Everything was neatly arranged and spotlessly clean, unlike the fishing sheds Shannon remembered from her youth. The lures were kept in glass-topped metal boxes, each in a separate compartment.

They enjoyed casting their lines and admiring each other's technique. The only problem was, neither caught a fish.

"With all this fancy equipment, you'd think they'd feel an obligation to bite," Shannon complained.

"It happens sometimes. That's when macho fishermen stop at the fish market on the way home. They won't admit they didn't catch anything."

"It's frustrating to see them right there in front of me—so near, but so elusive. It's tantalizing."

"Tell me about it."

"Well, I'm not willing to give up yet. I think I'll try that spot over there." Shannon waded to the middle of the stream and started to climb on a rock.

"I wouldn't do that. Those rocks are slip—" His advice stopped abruptly as she began to teeter.

Michel reached her in a couple of giant strides,

catching her before she fell into the water. Instead of lowering her to her feet, his arms remained around her, holding her tightly.

Shannon's breathless laughter died as she lifted her face and saw his expression. The raw desire in his eyes startled her, and her body stiffened instinctively.

He set her on her feet and then let go of her immediately. "I guess you discovered for yourself what I was about to tell you. Those rocks are slippery." He turned and waded to shore.

"Michel! I didn't mean—"

"It's all right. No harm done. I think it's time for lunch."

In an unguarded moment, Shannon had been about to say she didn't mean to pull away. Was that why he didn't let her finish? He was afraid it would be a replay of that night on the terrace. Would it have been?

She trailed after him to a shady spot under a tree, where he'd left the picnic basket. Shannon watched in silence as he unpacked one container after another. His chef had prepared every kind of delicacy for them.

"Oh, good, here are those rolled sandwiches I like," he said. "I knew Armand wouldn't forget. Try one, and some of this goose pâté." He took a foil-wrapped package out of a cooler.

Shannon nibbled on a truffle-topped deviled egg, instead, still trying to get over the awkward moment in the stream. But eventually she sampled most of the other food and drank the excellent dry white wine that Michel uncorked.

After they were through eating and had packed

away the remains, he asked, "What now? Another try for the elusive fish, or a hike through the grounds?"

"A hike, definitely. I have to walk off that elegant lunch."

They strolled down a gravel path that angled across the lawn. The path split when it reached a weathered sundial resting on a granite base.

"Which way do you want to go?" Michel asked. "The path on the right takes us along the bank next to the brook. The other one goes through the woods."

"Let's take that one. We've already been down by the water."

The gravel gave way to a mossy trail that was easier to walk on. As they went deeper into the woods, Shannon became enchanted with all the flora and fauna. A glimpse of wild violets or an occasional squirrel made her exclaim excitedly.

Michel watched her indulgently. "One would almost think you'd never been for a walk in the country before."

"There's not much undeveloped land in Los Angeles. They even paved over the orange groves nearby."

"That seems shocking. Perhaps you should move to Bonaventure, where we have our priorities straight."

"I'll certainly take it under advisement and get back to you." She kept her tone as light as his had been.

The trail suddenly widened into a charming glade with a rustic bench. They sat down to enjoy the lovely spot, but Shannon bounced up a moment later.

"Look over there, Michel! Those look like raspberries." She pointed to a tall tangle of vines a few yards off the trail. "Is that how they grow?"

"Don't tell me you've never seen wild raspberries?"

"How would I? Mine come in little cardboard trays from the supermarket. I want to pick some."

"Be careful. They're full of thorns."

She plunged into the woods and sampled the berries, calling back to tell him how delicious they were and urging him to join her.

"I'll take your word for it," he called back.

"Oh! Ow!" she exclaimed suddenly. "You were right about the thorns. One got me on the cheek. It really hurts!"

"Come out of there immediately!" Michel ordered.

"I'm trying, but I'm caught on the thorns."

"I'll come in and get you."

"No, it's okay." There was the sound of ripping cloth. "I'm free now." Shannon stumbled out of the woods and sank down on the moss to pull some stickers out of her hands.

Michel knelt beside her and dabbed at her cheek with a clean white handkerchief. "You're bleeding! We'd better go back to the lodge and wash that off."

"It's just a scratch. Help me get the leaves out of my hair." She turned her face away him.

Her long tangle of bright hair was spangled with leaves and bits of twigs. When Michel didn't start to pick them out, or even answer her, Shannon turned back to look at him.

His molten expression alerted her. She looked down and realized for the first time that the buttons of her shirt had been torn off and her bra was ripped open. His gaze was riveted on her bare breasts. Shannon was frozen in place. She knew it was imperative to cover herself, yet she was incapable of moving a muscle.

"Oh, darling, don't do this to me," Michel groaned, reaching out involuntarily.

"I didn't do it on purpose," she whispered.

"I know, but that doesn't make it any easier. You don't know how utterly irresistible you are." He pulled the two sides of her shirt closed.

As his hands brushed against her breasts, Shannon shivered with pleasure. She wanted more than that tantalizing touch, much more. She lifted her face and gazed up at him, parting her lips.

Michel caught his breath and lowered his head until their lips were inches apart. "I hope I'm not getting the wrong message," he murmured.

Her eyes never left his. "Doesn't your experience with women give you the answer?"

"I've never met a woman like you," he muttered. Then, as her body became liquid with anticipation, his hands closed almost painfully over her shoulders, holding her away. "This isn't what you really want. It wasn't the other night, and it still isn't. It's just the provocative situation we stumbled into. I can't take advantage of that."

Was Michel right? Shannon had told herself all those things and tried to convince herself that they were true. But she finally had to admit what she'd been denying for so long. She was head-over-heels, crazy in love with this man.

Nothing could come of it; she realized that. Yet if this was all she'd ever have, she would take it. It was better than having regrets for the rest of her life, knowing what she had given up without ever having experienced it fully.

Linking her arms loosely around his neck, she smiled enchantingly. "You're the most difficult man I've ever tried to seduce."

His tortured expression eased and he stared at her intently. When he received the answer he was looking for, the glow returned to his eyes. "I can't believe you had to try very hard."

"It's results that count," she murmured. "Am I getting through to you?"

"Does this answer your question?"

Michel took her in his arms and kissed her with pent-up hunger. His mouth devoured hers, while one hand tangled in her long, golden hair, holding her as though afraid she would change her mind.

That never even occured to her. She was committed now, and eager to know all he could teach her. The thought of the many, varied ways he could please her made her pulse race. Michel had kissed her before, but never with this unleashed, almost primitive passion. She wound her arms tightly around his neck and returned his kiss enthusiastically.

Her response delighted him. "You're so warm, so giving, my little angel. I want to make it wonderful for you."

"It already is," she whispered.

"It gets better," he promised, lowering his head to kiss one breast and then the other.

Shannon arched her body with a cry of excitement that kept building with every erotic caress.

"You're so exquisite," he said in a husky voice. "I want to touch every glorious inch of you."

He removed her tattered shirt and bra and unzipped her jeans. She lifted her hips to help him slide them down her legs. When she was left with only a pair of brief nylon panties, Michel straddled her body and gazed down at her with eyes as brilliant as the sun. Shannon couldn't look at him. Her eyelashes fanned her flushed cheeks, and she twisted her legs together.

"Never be shy with me, darling. You're beautiful all over, don't you know that?"

He hooked his fingers in the elastic of her panties and removed them. Then he gently parted her legs and leaned down to kiss the soft skin of her inner thigh.

"Oh, Michel," she breathed, "I've never felt this…this…" She couldn't think of words to describe it.

"It's all right." He smiled. "The look on your face is enough."

She held out her arms to him. "Make love to me, darling."

"It will be an honor and a pleasure."

Michel rose and stripped off his clothes in a blur of motion. He returned swiftly and covered her body with his, clasping her tightly. The erotic sensation made her greedy for more and she moved restlessly beneath him.

His breathing quickened and he said, "You're the answer to all my prayers." Before she could say anything, he entered her.

Shannon stiffened initially and uttered a smothered

little cry. Michel raised his head and gave her a shocked look. For an instant, both were motionless.

Then he said, "Why didn't you tell me?"

When he started to withdraw, she put her legs around his hips and pulled his mouth against hers. Michel's body remained rigid for a long moment, then it relaxed and he held her close.

Shannon's initial stab of pain was replaced by a throbbing heat in her loins that grew in intensity. She moved, tentatively at first, then with greater urgency.

Michel's movements were also restrained, almost reluctant, but his passion soon rose to meet hers. Their damp bodies came together, then parted, only to come together again in a sensuous dance that grew wilder as they climbed to the peak of sensual satisfaction.

Shannon reached it first. Michel held her tightly as wave after wave of delight swept through her. Only then did he take his own reward.

She was blissfully relaxed afterward, still enjoying the diminishing throbs of pleasure that were warm reminders of the ecstasy they'd shared. She wanted to remain joined like this to Michel, but he levered himself off her.

When Shannon finally found the energy to open her eyes, he was sitting a short distance away, staring at her. Her smile faltered as she noticed the expression on his face. It almost looked like anger!

"Why didn't you tell me you were a virgin?" he demanded. "How could you let me make love to you?"

Chapter Ten

Shannon couldn't believe Michel's reaction. She thought he had been as moved by their shared experience as she was. Well, chalk it up to experience—or lack of, in her case.

"I'm sorry if you were disappointed," she said stiffly.

"That's not what I said! Why didn't you tell me you were a virgin?"

"I didn't think it made any difference."

"You didn't think—" He sprang to his feet and ran his fingers through his thick hair. "I have never in my life taken a girl's innocence!"

"I'm a woman, not a girl. And you didn't seduce me. I chose to have sex." She purposely didn't call it "making love," although it was for her. But he must never discover that.

"Lucky me," Michel said. "Can you tell me why I was the chosen one? Was it because of my title?"

"No! I—" His sarcastic tone almost made her blurt out the truth, that she'd fallen in love with him. Shannon took a deep breath. "You're experienced enough to know that I was attracted to you."

"I can't believe I'm the first man you felt that way about."

"Believe whatever you like." She reached for her clothes and pulled them on hurriedly, hoping he would do the same. Michel's lean, nude body still affected her powerfully, in spite of her hurt and disillusionment.

To her relief, he pulled on his briefs and jeans, but he continued to search for answers. "I'm sorry I was so abrupt," he said in a milder tone. "If you'd only told me, this would never have happened."

"It doesn't matter," she mumbled, lowering her head and holding together the edges of her torn shirt.

"It matters a great deal." He lifted her chin, forcing her to face him. "Your first time should have been special, with a man you love."

It *had* been special—until now. Shannon's eyes filled with tears.

"For God's sake, don't cry!" He took her in his arms and held her tightly for just a moment before putting her away. "I feel badly enough."

"Let it go, Michel. There's nothing either of us can do about it now. We'd better leave. Do you have a T-shirt or something that I can wear back to the castle? I'd like to answer as few questions as possible about today."

"Of course. I'll find something for you." He didn't

start back to the lodge, however. After staring at her moodily, he said, "I suppose the honorable thing to do would be to offer to marry you, but we would both regret it."

Shannon was wounded by his dispassionate tone. What he meant was, he would regret it. "I never expected you to marry me! Is that what this is all about? You're afraid I'll make a fuss, and you'll get some bad publicity?"

"I didn't mean to imply—"

"Well, you did, and you're way off base! I don't need to trap anybody into marrying me."

"That's obvious." His eyes lingered on her lovely face.

"And don't try to flatter me. Your famous charm isn't going to work this time. What happened today was a mistake, obviously, but I didn't have any ulterior motive. I wouldn't marry you even if you asked me! Why would I want to live in this little out-of-the-way country? You're not *that* charming."

"I've hurt you, and I apologize," he said quietly. "When I said we would both have regrets, it wasn't for the reason you think. During the time we've spent together, you've talked about wanting a large family."

"What's that got to do with anything?"

"I can't father a child."

Shannon stared at him in shock, not sure she had heard correctly. Then disbelief set in. Michel was the most virile man she'd ever known. He must be saying that to spare her feelings. But would any man lie about what might be considered a reflection on his manhood?

"It isn't something I'd make up," he said wryly, reading her mind. "I was as shocked as you are when I found out."

"Did something happen? I mean, was it a childhood disease like mumps, or something like that?"

"No, I found out quite by accident. My horse stumbled during a polo match. I wasn't hurt, but the doctors insisted on a complete physical, X rays, blood tests and all the rest. During a routine test they discovered that my sperm count is so low that I must give up the expectation of ever having children."

"There have to be specialists for that sort of thing."

"Believe me, we've explored every possibility. I was tested regularly for a time, but nothing changed. Finally I accepted the fact it wasn't going to. I was only tormenting myself. The doctors are the only ones who know about my condition, and they've been sworn to secrecy. I'd appreciate it if you'd also respect my confidence."

"Of course!"

"I haven't even told my brother, although Devon will have to know sooner or later. I plan to abdicate in his favor as soon as he becomes engaged."

"Oh, no! You're such a fine ruler. Devon told me how much your people love you."

"He'll make an equally good monarch, once the torch is passed. Devon isn't as frivolous as he seems. I have great faith in him."

"It seems like such a shame."

"Nobody said life was fair." Michel smiled faintly. "I told you this because I owed it to you. I did you a great disservice today, I didn't want to take away your self-esteem, as well.''

So, he damaged his own instead. Shannon felt like crying, but she swallowed her tears. ''If it's any help, I don't regret what happened today. You have nothing to feel sorry about. Nobody could have made my first experience more meaningful.''

''Don't, Shannon.'' A look of pain crossed his face. ''Let's go back to the lodge and I'll find something for you to wear.''

Shannon was glad they returned before Marcie and Devon. She wasn't up to making small talk after all that had happened.

She ran a bath in the deep marble tub that was part of the renovation Michel had done throughout the castle. The large bathroom also had pink marble floors, mirrored walls and a chandelier instead of a ceiling fixture. It was enough to delight any woman, but Shannon was sunk in despair.

She should be cuddling in Michel's arms right now, whispering playfully together as he aroused her sleeping passions with his knowledgeable hands. Her body heated at the remembrance and she quickly slid into the water.

Would Michel have asked her to marry him if it hadn't been for his problem? He must care about her, or he wouldn't have entrusted her with a secret he'd even kept from his brother.

That was just wishful thinking, she reflected sadly. Michel had told her the reason, and it wasn't that he cared. He felt he owed it to her. If he *had* asked her to marry him, it would have been out of a sense of honor, not love.

Could she have accepted his proposal, even if one had been forthcoming? On the rare occasions when she'd thought about getting married, the groom's face was always shadowy, but the rest of the picture was clear. She saw herself surrounded by little toddlers who would climb into her lap and shower her with kisses.

Could she give up that dream? It would be a huge sacrifice. She would have to think long and hard before making such a momentous decision. Not that she had to. Michel hadn't asked her to marry him. He'd merely explained why he couldn't.

Unlike Shannon, Michel tried to put the traumatic afternoon out of his mind. He went to his office and began to review the conditions of a pending trade agreement.

The legal language required concentration, but he kept seeing Shannon's expressive face on the stapled pages, sometimes laughing mischievously, other times softly radiant.

Michel groaned. Why hadn't he realized how innocent she was? But how could he have known that a woman so exquisite was also chaste? He cursed himself for that moment when she had cried out inadvertently and he had known.

But then she had twined her arms and legs around him so he couldn't stop. What difference would it have made, though? The damage was already done. At least he had made it a pleasurable experience for her.

He was knowledgeable enough to know that. Michel's loins tightened as he remembered her body moving eagerly under his, her little cries of rapture as he fed her passion. He had made sure that she was completely satisfied. Didn't that count for something?

What about your own satisfaction? he thought derisively. The inexpressible feeling of being enveloped in her warmth, the throbbing joy of her answering thrusts. Then the final release when the fury subsided and they floated gently back to earth.

Michel pushed back his chair abruptly and went over to stare out the window. This was exactly why he didn't want to get involved. Shannon was inexperienced, she was naive, they had different values. A husband would never be important to her unless he could give her children. Had he expected her to say it didn't matter? That was pretty unrealistic. She'd made her priorities clear from the beginning.

Not that either of them wanted to get married, Michel told himself impatiently. He was just sorry that things had gotten out of hand and ended so badly.

Devon came into the office after a brief knock. "You and Shannon should have been with us today, Michel. The Wainwrights' party after the dog show was a blast! Their Irish wolfhound, King Seamus of Maltsby, won best in show, so we were all celebrating. That dog would scare Attila the Hun, but he's a real pussycat."

"That's nice."

Devon didn't notice his brother's preoccupation. "How was your day at the lodge? Did you manage to scare up some excitement for Shannon, although I don't know what could happen up there."

"Don't you have something to do, Devon? I'm trying to get a little work done here."

"When aren't you?"

It was just an offhand comment, but Michel's temper flared. "One of us has to, and you're not about to take any of the responsibility, in spite of your offer last night."

"Give me a chance. You have to tell me what you want me to do," Devon protested. "Not busywork, something that will really make your life a little easier."

Michel was immediately remorseful. He was taking out his frustration on his best friend and ally. "Forgive me. I'm feeling the pressure of the summit meeting in Paris, but I should be able to handle it better. They're a regular occurrence."

Devon tried to hide his concern. "Why don't you take a couple of weeks off after the meeting? Go sailing off Mykonos, or lie on the beach at Cannes," he suggested in a casual voice.

"There's nothing wrong with me." Michel managed a smile. "I told you that yesterday, and I didn't develop a terminal disease overnight."

"Don't talk that way! I need to have you around."

"I'll be here." Michel walked back to his desk and picked up the bulky report he'd been trying to concentrate on, hoping to end the conversation.

It worked. Devon said, "I'll see you tonight, then. We're meeting a lot of the people from the party at the Waverly Club. Freddie is arranging for a private room."

"You'll have to convey my regrets. I can't make it tonight."

"You told me just last night that you intended to spend more time with us. What happened today to change your mind? Did you and Shannon have another dustup?"

"I don't appreciate having my conduct questioned." Michel's stormy face should have alerted his brother.

But Devon was too consumed with his own annoyance to heed the warning signals. "The only thing I'm questioning is why you two can't get along for more than a minute and a half. I swear, you both act like a couple of teenagers!"

Michel drew himself up to his full, impressive height. "When I want your opinion, I will ask for it. Now leave my office and don't come back unless I send for you."

Marcie at least was looking forward to the evening when she showed up at Shannon's suite in the late afternoon. "Your hair looks really great! You'll be a hit at dinner tonight." She filled Shannon in on their plans, then continued. "Devon told me Michel can't make it, but you two are probably all talked out anyway. Did you have a good time today? What did you do?" she asked. "It was very nice. We went fishing," she added, when "nice" didn't seem to be enough.

"Whatever turns you on." Marcie shrugged. "You really missed a fun afternoon. Everybody asked where you and Michel were."

"They're his friends. I'm sure nobody missed *me*."

"Are you kidding? You're a local celebrity." Marcie slanted a glance at her, while remarking innocently, "It's a good thing you'll be with us for dinner, since Michel won't. If neither of you showed up tonight, people might think there was something hot and heavy going on between you two."

Shannon had considered declining the invitation. After the day she'd spent, it would be difficult to act happy and carefree. But she'd have to bite the bullet. The last thing she wanted was for his friends to start speculating about Michel and herself.

"People are always dreaming up romances that don't exist," Shannon said dismissively. "What shall I wear tonight? How dressy will it be?"

"These people always get dressed up, but it's just dinner, not a formal affair. Let's go look in your closet."

After much debate they chose coral-colored silk pants and a matching silk knit top with a scooped neck. Spike heels and a large, beaded silk butterfly fastened to a satin choker completed the outfit.

"Perfect!" Marcie declared. "Understated yet elegant. Wear your hair long and loose like that, too. It looks sexy. The men will love it. Too bad Michel won't be there to see them drool."

"Why would I care what he thinks?" Shannon asked coolly. "I hope *you* don't think there is anything going on between us?"

"Well, you do behave like lovers or, at least, a couple who are very attracted to each other. I mean, one day you're as close as two pieces of Velcro, and the next day the atmosphere is so chilly a person could get frostbite standing next to you."

"You're imagining things."

"Is Devon imagining things, too?"

"Have you been discussing me with him?" Shannon asked in outrage.

"I wouldn't call it a discussion," Marcie explained carefully. "We both noticed that you and Michel seem to argue a lot. We couldn't help wondering why. I don't suppose you'd like to tell me?"

"It isn't important enough to talk about. There is nothing romantic involved. We've just been together too much. I guess we're getting on each other's nerves. Michel did me a favor by deciding not to go tonight."

"Well, as long as you're okay with it. I wouldn't want an unhappy love affair to spoil the great time you've had up until now."

"Not to worry. I'm going to have an even better time without Michel. Will there be any interesting men at the dinner tonight?"

"There's always Devon."

"I wouldn't poach on your territory."

"Devon and I are just pals. Maybe in the beginning I hoped something would develop, but he's not ready to get serious about anybody, and I'm not either." Marcie looked at her watch. "If I hurry, I'll have time to wash my hair. See you later."

Shannon took great pains with her hair and makeup. She was determined to look her best and pretend she was having a ball. If Marcie and Devon had both noticed a difference in her, she'd have to change her image. It would be mortifying to have Michel think she attached any importance to what happened today .

After all her primping and tweaking, she was a few

minutes late getting downstairs. The other two were already waiting in the entry.

"You look great," Devon told her.

"Thanks to Marcie," Shannon said. "She chose my outfit."

Before he could comment, Michel came racing down the grand staircase. He was trying to fasten an onyx cuff link, so he didn't see their little group until he reached the bottom of the stairs.

"What's the hurry, Michel?" Devon would have remarked that he was pretty dressed up for a night of working at his desk, but Shannon's feelings were more important than getting back at his brother.

Michel didn't answer. He was staring at Shannon as though he hadn't seen her for days. "You look lovely," he said finally.

"Thank you. It's the outfit. Clothes make all the difference." What she'd meant to be a light remark backfired. Her breathing quickened when she remembered where her clothes had landed that afternoon.

Marcie quickly stepped in to smooth over whatever was wrong. "You look pretty good yourself," she told Michel. "Doesn't he, Devon?"

"Don't ask me. I'm just his brother. I don't get to voice an opinion."

As a look of impatience crossed Michel's strong face, a beautiful blonde came out of the library down the hall. Her hair was perfect, every strand in place, and her outfit was high style and expensive.

"What's keeping you, Michel?" she called. "I swear, you men take longer to get dressed than we women do."

When she reached them, he introduced her as Margarite, the duchess of Beauvoix.

They exchanged a few words, then she said to Devon, ''Aren't you proud of me? I persuaded your brother to come out and party with us tonight.''

''You'll have to tell me your secret,'' Devon drawled.

''I convinced him that all work and no play is injurious to one's health,'' she said with a tinkling little laugh.

''Devon already subscribes to that theory,'' Michel remarked .

The tension in the entry hall was palpable. It eased somewhat when a man came out of the library looking for Margarite. Shannon recognized him as one of the men she'd met at the dinner dance here at the castle. His name was Terrence something, or maybe it was Wesley.

He came toward them with a pleased look on his face. ''I hope you're all joining us tonight. The more the merrier.''

''Sorry, but we have another engagement,'' Devon said.

''You'll have more fun with us. Tell him, Michel.''

Margarite spoke up quickly. ''Don't be a pest, Terrence. It's not polite to break a previous engagement.'' She linked her arm through Michel's, making it clear that he was her date for the night.

''Hadn't we better get going?'' Marcie asked.

''You're right, we should,'' Devon agreed.

They milled around for a few minutes longer, saying goodbye and mentioning future plans.

''Sorry you won't be with us tonight, but I'll see

you tomorrow night, anyway.'' Terrence smiled at Shannon. ''At the de Forests','' he added, when she looked blank.

''They're having a barbecue,'' Devon said. ''Didn't I mention it?''

''You should have, it's in Shannon's honor—and yours too, of course, Michel. Mimi de Forest has gone to a lot of trouble to make it authentic, just like the ones in Texas.''

''What fun!'' Marcie gave him a mischievous smile. ''Will we have hot dogs and hamburgers?''

''Are you getting tired of caviar?'' Devon teased.

Michel had been stirring restlessly. His gaze kept flicking to Shannon, then away. Finally he said, ''Will you round up the others, Terrence? Tell them we're ready to leave.''

''We should be going, too,'' Devon said.

The group broke up as he and the two women went outside. Two limousines were waiting at the curb, one in back of the other.

''I feel like I'm at a movie premiere,'' Marcie commented. When they were all seated, she asked, ''Is Mimi really having a barbecue? Somehow, I can't picture this crowd in jeans and cotton shirts.''

''I don't know what the dress code will be,'' Devon said. ''To my knowledge, this is the first time anyone has attempted something like this.''

''It should be an experience. Right, Shannon?''

''What? Oh, yes, I'm looking forward to it,'' she said vaguely.

She hadn't really been listening. The unexpected meeting with Michel had shaken her more than she expected. She could tell he was uncomfortable, too, although not for the same reason. At least this meeting had been brief, but what if he felt obligated to attend the barbecue tomorrow night? The thought of spending a whole evening in his company was insupportable!

"I don't suppose Michel will be able to come tomorrow night," she said in what she hoped was a casual voice. "He must be booked up weeks in advance, and Mimi's affair is sort of last-minute."

"That's true," Devon said. "Invitations to these things are usually sent out weeks in advance because people have such busy agendas. It's a tribute to you that everybody is so eager to entertain you that they're willing to rearrange their social calendars to fit your time limitations."

"They're the nicest people I've ever met," Shannon said with sincerity. "I'm sure Mimi will understand that Michel had a previous engagement. I certainly understand."

"I don't know what his appointment book looks like. I'm just his brother. But I can assure you that Michel will put in an appearance, even if he doesn't stay long. It would be insulting to Mimi if he didn't."

Marcie was looking at him thoughtfully. "Did you and Michel have a row? You two seemed to have such a great relationship. You always acted more like friends than brothers."

"It isn't nice to pry into someone's personal life, Marcie," Shannon chided.

"It's all right," Devon said. "I'm the one who was impolite. I shouldn't have sniped at Michel the way I did."

"He got in a few jabs at you, too," Marcie remarked with a grin.

"And I'm sure he's as sorry about it as I am. Michel has a quick temper, but he gets over it just as quickly. We'll apologize to each other and the whole thing will be forgotten. By tomorrow night everything will be back to normal."

"Between the two brothers," Shannon thought somberly. Nothing would ever be the same again between herself and Michel.

Chapter Eleven

Shannon had breakfast in her suite the next morning. She didn't think Michel would show up in the dining room—he was just as anxious as she to avoid a meeting—but she didn't want to take any chances. Tonight would be bad enough.

Devon had to appear at a fund-raiser that day, and Marcie decided not to accompany him. She and Shannon went shopping instead.

"This social whirl is fun, but we've hardly spent any time together," Marcie said. "Today will be like old times."

"Don't pretend you chose to be with me," Shannon teased. "Devon probably told you the fund-raiser would be dull."

"He always says that," Marcie laughed. "But I enjoy them. I think he does, too. He just won't admit it."

"You're going to miss all the excitement, aren't you?"

"Who wouldn't want to live like this?"

"It's very nice, but I'll be glad to get back to normal," Shannon said, even as she wondered if that would ever be possible.

"You have more to go back to than I do. But when you start telling people about all the fabulous experiences you had here, you'll be homesick for Bonaventure."

"It's possible." Shannon didn't want to talk about it. "Let's look at those scarves over there. They would make nice gifts to take home, don't you think?"

Marcie refused to be distracted. "Have you ever thought about living here?"

"You're joking!"

"Think about it. No more crowds and fighting for parking spaces. No more standing in line for everything. What's so great about living in a megalopolis?"

"It isn't for everybody, I'll agree. But if you're fed up with Los Angeles, then move to a small town. People who feel stressed out don't go all the way to another continent!" Shannon exclaimed.

"Why not, if they found Shangri-la there?"

"You might have. I didn't," Shannon answered tersely.

"You said it was a little piece of paradise, until you and Michel had a falling-out. I don't know what it was about, but you both have tempers, and—"

"I don't have a temper," Shannon interrupted indignantly. "*He* does!"

"Okay, then let's just say you're both spoiled. Michel is a ruling prince, so he's used to getting his own way, and you've always had men knocking themselves out to please you, so you expect him to follow the pattern. It's predictable that neither of you would give an inch if you had a disagreement."

"You don't know what you're talking about," Shannon muttered.

"And you don't feel like telling me." Marcie paused, but when Shannon didn't enlighten her, she said, "Whatever it was, if you stayed on here, I'm sure it would all blow over. And who knows what might develop? You two would be a perfect couple."

"Who put you up to this—Devon?" Shannon knew it wasn't Michel.

Marcie sighed. "No, it was my own idea and I knew it probably wouldn't work, but I had to try."

"Why?"

"Because I'm going to miss you. I'm not going home with you at the end of the week."

"You and Devon…" Shannon said uncertainly.

"No, it's nothing like that. It's something equally exciting, though."

"Wait! Let's go someplace for coffee. I need to be sitting down for this kind of news."

They found a little tearoom, and took a booth in a quiet corner. After they'd ordered, Shannon said, "Now, tell me everything. How could you keep something like this a secret from me until the last minute?"

"I honestly didn't think it would happen. You know how it is. When you want something so badly, you tell yourself it's just pie-in-the-sky, because you don't want to be disappointed.''

"Are you ever going to tell me?" Shannon demanded.

"Okay." Marcie laughed. "You know how everybody has been so complimentary about the jewelry I make? Those women at the dinner dance were the first, but since then a lot more women have been asking me to make things for them. I'd love to be a jewelry designer, but I never thought I could make a living at it."

Shannon didn't want to trample on her cousin's dream, but she was afraid it was impractical. "Do you think you can get enough business from Devon's friends to support yourself?" she asked carefully.

"I know I couldn't. But I met a man at one of the parties recently—Pierre Larousse. He owns a chain of upscale boutiques throughout the Continent. Someone told him about my jewelry, and he said nice things about the pieces I was wearing. I thought he was just being polite, but he asked me to make some sketches for him and send them to his hotel ASAP. I didn't think anything would come of it, but I didn't have anything to lose, so I sent them. He called me this morning to say he loved the sketches and he wants me to design an entire line! He's going to put my jewelry in all his boutiques."

"That's fantastic! But when did you have time to do all that work?"

"You'll make time for a chance like this. I got up early in the morning and worked for a couple of hours before breakfast, and again at night after I got home."

"You really deserve this break," Shannon said fondly. "I'm so happy for you."

"I just wish I could persuade you to stay, too. I'll miss you like crazy."

"I'll miss you, too. But after you become a famous designer you can afford to come home for visits whenever you like." Shannon ignored the part about her moving to Bonaventure.

Devon came to greet the two women when he heard Jennings open the front door for them. "I don't see enough packages to justify all those hours of shopping," he joked.

"Shopping is a female bonding ritual," Marcie told him. "It has nothing to do with buying things. Men don't understand that."

"It isn't the only thing we don't understand about women. Right, Michel?" His brother was crossing the entry to go upstairs.

Courtesy demanded that Michel stop and chat for a few moments. "I can't quarrel with that," he said with a forced smile.

"Women have just as much trouble understanding men." Shannon spoke up suddenly. She was getting tired of taking his little digs without striking back. "They can always find something to complain about."

After a beat of silence, Marcie said, "I know one thing these two won't complain about. We can all wear jeans tonight."

Shannon waited for Michel to say he wasn't going to the party. Or at least, that he was taking his own car because he couldn't stay long. But Devon was evidently right; Michel didn't have an acceptable excuse for not attending.

"Marcie assures me that jeans are the proper attire for a barbecue," Devon said.

"Whether they're correct or not, I'm wearing them," Michel stated. "It's the only good thing about this evening." After realizing how that sounded, he said, "What I meant was, I don't care for these cutesy theme parties. The hostess usually has activities planned that involve guest participation."

"Are you afraid she's going to hand you a stick and expect you to toast your own marshmallows over a bonfire?" Marcie teased.

"Good Lord! You don't think she would, do you?"

"Don't worry, that's one of my many talents. I'll toast yours for you."

"We'll all take care of you," Devon said. "We know you don't have the common touch."

"And you do?" Michel scoffed, but in a joking way.

The two men had clearly made up their differences. Shannon was glad, because she had a feeling their argument was over her.

It was the only thing she had to feel good about, she thought as she dressed for the party that night. Shannon couldn't help feeling melancholy. Her formerly happy life was disintegrating, bit by bit. Marcie's announcement that she wasn't going home was the final blow. Well, look on the bright side, at least nothing else can happen, Shannon told herself.

The de Forest estate was only a short distance from the castle. The exterior of the large chateau was formidable, but the interior was gracious and exquisitely furnished, although they only caught a glimpse of the many drawing and sitting rooms. A butler led them outside where the party was being held.

The de Forests had gone to a lot of trouble to create what they thought was an authentic barbecue. On a section of the vast lawn, several large grills were lined up in a row with a white-garbed chef presiding over each one.

A bar was set up a short distance away, attended by two bartenders. Umbrella tables were spotted over the lawn, and waiters circulated to take drink orders.

"You won't need me after all," Marcie teased Michel. "You're in no danger of having to do anything for yourself. I'll bet there's even somebody to cut your meat for you."

"Don't hostesses provide that service at your parties?" he asked with a straight face.

Their host and hostess came over to greet them. They were dressed casually, but not in jeans. Mimi inspected Shannon's outfit with interest. Shannon was wearing a pair of jeans and a powder-blue silk T-shirt.

"I love that top!" she said. "I've never seen one like it here." She stared at the large orchid blossom silk screened across Shannon's left shoulder.

They were all looking at her, but Shannon was most conscious of Michel's intense gaze. She was aware of the fact that the silk knit clung to her body, outlining her breasts.

"I'll be glad to send you one when I get home," she told Mimi. "I got it at a little boutique near my office."

"How very kind of you, my dear!"

As they discussed European sizes and the corresponding ones in America, the men drifted away, to Shannon's great relief. If Michel would just keep his distance, they would both manage to get through this. The grounds were certainly big enough. With any luck, they might not have to say another word to each other all evening.

Some women joined their group, and then several of the men. The conversation was light and pleasant, typical party talk with a lot of bantering and laughter. Shannon could have enjoyed herself if she weren't so conscious of Michel.

Sometimes when she looked up he was staring at her, but most of the time he was smiling and talking with some young woman or another who was listening with a rapt look on her face. Shannon forced herself to pay attention to her own group.

Mimi was saying, "This is the first barbecue I've ever given, but certainly not the last. I've had such fun arranging all the little details. The guests seem to be enjoying the novelty, too."

"Why not?" Marcie murmured to Shannon as two waiters with silver trays offered hot and cold hors d'oeuvres. "This is the same service they get at any other lawn party."

It was a long cocktail hour, but eventually Gerry de Forest banged a rod on a metal triangle and announced that dinner was served. Guests began to wander over to the umbrella tables to look at the place cards.

As they headed for the nearest table, Marcie and Shannon exchanged an amused look over the incongruity of place cards at a barbecue.

Mimi intercepted them before they could look for their names. "No, you and Marcie are at the two head tables over by the fountain," she said.

Shannon had a chilling premonition, which turned out to be correct. She and Michel were seated next to each other, and there was nothing she could do about it. Marcie wasn't even at their table. Devon was presiding over the other head table, with her beside him.

"Since I'm the host, I get to sit with the prince and princess," Gerry said jovially, holding Shannon's chair for her. "There you are," he said as Michel arrived. "I was taking over your duties until you got here."

"That was very thoughtful of you. I'm afraid I've been neglecting Shannon."

"I didn't notice," she said. "Mimi and I were having a most interesting conversation."

"Women enjoy talking to each other more than they do to us," one of the men at the table observed. "It's very deflating to a chap's ego."

"It shouldn't be," a woman laughed. "We talk about men—the same as you fellows talk about women."

Under cover of the general conversation, Michel said to Shannon in a low voice, "I'm sorry that you feel uncomfortable."

"No more than you do," she answered.

It was torture to sit this close to Michel and still be separated by a chasm as wide as the Grand Canyon. She longed to wipe out the bitterness between them, to see his eyes lit by desire and feel his hot mouth moving seductively over hers. Perhaps the cruelest torture was knowing those things would never happen again.

Fortunately the waiters began serving their first course, chilled vichyssoise. She had to smile at the crystal bowls in their silver holders.

"I hope Mimi never goes to a real, American-style barbecue," Shannon commented.

"I suppose this bears no resemblance?"

"Well, let's just say, I can't imagine her holding an ear of buttery corn, or gnawing on a rib dripping with sauce."

Michel returned her smile. "It does rather boggle the mind. But she meant well. Mimi was trying to please you."

"She did! I wasn't criticizing her. Your friends are the nicest people I've ever met."

"You see? There *are* some things you like about Bonaventure."

"I never said I didn't like it here."

"Shall I refresh your memory? I believe your precise words were, 'Why would I want to live in this little out-of-the-way country?'"

Shannon remembered exactly when she'd made that statement. It was after their lovemaking had ended so disastrously and she had lashed out at him from pain and rejection.

"You have a good memory," she said, gazing down at her soup so she wouldn't have to look at him.

"It's a curse, put on me by a bad fairy when I was born."

Did that mean he didn't want to remember her? Or he preferred not to remember the aftermath? She raised her eyes to scan his face, but the waiters were back.

One removed their soup dishes, and a second man replaced them with delicate porcelain dinner plates. Then a procession of waiters offered platters of sliced sirloin steak charred from the grill. The meat was surrounded by an assortment of artfully arranged vegetables.

The charged moment with Michel was diffused during all the activity, and after that the conversation became general.

They were finished with dinner when their host rose and held up his glass. "I want to propose a toast to our American princess, who was the inspiration for tonight's festivities."

They all raised their wineglasses in enthusiastic participation.

"Would you like to say a few words, Shannon?" Gerry asked.

She rose and said, "Yes, I'm glad to have this opportunity to thank you and everyone here for the warm hospitality you've all shown me, a complete stranger. I also want to thank Michel for opening his castle to what surely must have seemed like a foreign invasion. After the shock wore off he was very gracious about it, though. He rarely lost his temper." She was interrupted by knowing laughter. "But I don't have to tell you people how patient he is." The laughter grew so boisterous that guests at the other tables looked over at them.

"You should hold on to this one, Michel," a man said. "She's more than just a pretty face."

Shannon's smile faltered for an instant, then she

continued, "I'm going to miss all of you, but I'm taking home a lot of wonderful memories." And some that aren't so great, she added silently. "I won't ever forget you."

"That sounds like a farewell speech," Gerry observed.

"I guess you could call it that. I'm leaving on Sunday."

The comments came from all sides. "It can't be two weeks already."

"It seems as if you just got here!"

"If Michel is putting you out, you can stay with us." This came from Gerry.

"I'd be happy to have her stay as long as she likes," Michel said, but Shannon knew he realized it was expected of him.

"It's nice to be wanted, but it's wise to leave while people still feel that way," she joked.

At the next table, Mimi was calling for everybody's attention. "I have an announcement to make. We have something very different planned for this special evening. I've been told that Americans like to play games, so for your entertainment tonight, we're going to have a scavenger hunt. But don't worry, you won't have to drive around the countryside. Everything on your list is hidden right here on the grounds."

Waiters were threading their way through the tables distributing slips of paper and small cloisonné pens, which were party favors.

"You'll have one hour to find everything," Mimi continued. "At the end of that time we'll all meet back here for dessert, and to award the prizes. Gentlemen, the lady sitting on your right will be your partner.''

That meant Shannon and Michel would be a team. His face darkened as he read the list he'd been handed. Shannon soon discovered why. The theme of the scavenger hunt was love and marriage. The first item on the list was a love letter. Other items related to courtship, and toward the end was a wedding ring. The last article was a baby shoe.

Mimi must have been a dental school dropout in a previous life, Shannon thought despairingly. She couldn't have hit so many nerves if she'd tried!

Chapter Twelve

As the other guests scattered over the lawn, Michel said to Shannon, "Have you ever been on one of these things?"

"Not since high school. It was fun then."

She hadn't meant it as a criticism of his very evident reluctance. But he took it that way and attempted to change his attitude—on the surface, at least.

"I'm sure it will be fun this time, as well. You'll have to lead the way, since I'm a complete novice."

"That must be a novelty for you," Shannon couldn't help saying.

"Not really. I'm finding out there are a lot of things I don't do well." Without giving her a chance to comment, he said, "Where do we start?"

"Well..." She glanced at the list. "The corsage looks easiest. Why don't we start with that? It might be in plain sight on one of the bushes."

Michel's expression was dubious as he glanced around at the landscaped gardens. "There are flowers everywhere."

"Not with ribbons on them. You know how florists make up corsages with those big curly bows?"

"I've never observed the process firsthand."

"Oh, I forgot. You probably have a designated servant to order your flowers for you," she teased. "Such decadence! Do you even tie your own tie?"

"Does any man?" Michel asked with a smile.

Shannon's heart took a giant leap upward. This was almost like old times when they could joke back and forth without any underlying tension. It was too late to mend their relationship, but she'd settle now for just parting on good terms.

Once the ice was broken they started to enjoy themselves. They found the corsage tied to a rosebush, as Shannon had guessed. Then they found a blue satin garter masquerading as a collar around the neck of a statue of Cupid. But after that they began to talk about other things and gradually lost interest in the scavenger hunt. Eventually they just sat on a low wall surrounding a fish pond.

Michel and Shannon were scarcely conscious of the other guests scurrying by with their decorated tote bags, poking into shrubbery and under the cushions of lawn furniture. When comments were made that they were slacking off, they simply nodded absently.

After repeated remarks from the others, Shannon finally said, "The time must be almost up. I suppose we should start looking for some of the stuff on the list."

"Do you really want to?"

"No, I'm enjoying this."

"I am, too." His eyes were sad as he reached out and gently brushed a breeze-tossed strand of hair off her cheek.

The sensuous feeling of his fingers trailing across her skin made Shannon's pulse race. Her lips parted as they gazed into each other's eyes for a heart-stopping moment, oblivious to their surroundings or other people. They were alone in the universe.

Then Michel took a deep breath and lowered his hand. At the same moment, a discordant sound filled the air. Mimi was banging on the metal triangle that had summoned them to dinner. The scavenger hunt was over—along with everything else, Shannon told herself poignantly.

"I guess we disgraced ourselves," she said. "We only found two things."

"Well, at least it shows we tried."

Michel was so completely in command of himself that she might almost have imagined the regret in his eyes as he drew away. He certainly didn't feel the wrenching disappointment she did. Shannon gazed down at the path as they started back to the tables.

That was how she noticed a small blue object at the base of some tall delphiniums. It was partially covered by fallen blossoms almost the same color.

"Where are you going?" Michel asked as she walked over for a better look.

"I might have found one more item. Maybe we won't win the booby prize after all."

She hunched down and discovered a blue velvet jeweler's box. Inside, on a bed of white satin, was a simple gold band. Or at least, it looked like gold.

Shannon's initial reaction was the pleased surprise that comes from finding something unexpectedly. Then the significance of it hit her. There were bound to be comments about whoever found the wedding ring, especially if it were the two unmarried guests of honor. Michel might be able to handle it, but Shannon couldn't.

"What did you find?" He was walking toward her.

"I thought I saw something, but I was mistaken." She returned the box to its hiding place and stood hastily.

"It doesn't matter. I suppose technically the game is over anyway," he said.

"You're right, it is."

Something in her tone alerted him, and Michel glanced quickly at her. But they had reached the others, and everybody was chattering about what they'd found and where.

They all returned to their tables, where waiters were serving coffee and an elaborate ice-cream cake for dessert.

Mimi stood once more to determine the winner of the scavenger hunt. "Let's start with the first item on the list. Whoever has the love letter, please stand up and read it."

"Do we have to guess who wrote it?" somebody asked.

A young man at a back table called out, "If it's addressed to Occupant, we'll know it's from Michel. That saves our bachelor prince from mixing up the names of all his women."

The man had clearly had too much to drink, which surprised Shannon. Although wine was always served with dinner, and anything a guest desired was available during the cocktail hour, she had never seen anyone even slightly inebriated. From the shocked and disapproving looks all around, he wouldn't be invited back.

"That will do," Mimi said firmly.

"Hey, it wasn't a criticism. I'd pay a fortune for his address book!"

"I'd advise you to be very careful, Franklin." Michel's tight smile didn't fool anyone. "Court jesters used to meet an untimely end when they weren't funny."

A woman stood up hastily and said she and her partner had found the letter in the fork of a tree. It turned out to be a parody of a love letter. Everybody laughed and the distasteful incident appeared to have been smoothed over. But Shannon wasn't so sure. She could sense the tension in Michel's lean body.

Everyone else seemed to be enjoying the results of the scavenger hunt. Mimi checked off the items on her list as people displayed them. They were down to the next to the last one, but nobody claimed to have it.

"I must have hidden the wedding ring too well," Mimi said. "How annoying! It said in my game book that the person who found it would be the next bride or groom."

Shannon could have told her not to believe everything she read.

The party started to break up soon after the prizes were awarded. Shannon wasn't surprised that Michel was among the first to suggest leaving, although she was ready.

In the car on the way home, Marcie talked enthusiastically about what a great party it had been, and how super all the people were. "Are you sure you won't change your mind, Shannon?"

"About what?" Michel asked.

"Oops!" Marcie looked at Devon. "You didn't talk to him yet, did you?"

"Will someone please tell me what's going on?" Michel's handsome face wore its autocratic expression.

"It's nothing to worry about," Devon assured his brother. "Marcie has been presented with a business opportunity, and she isn't going home on Sunday."

Michel turned his head quickly to look at Shannon.

She couldn't see his expression in the shifting shadows inside the car, but she knew what it would be. "Don't worry, *I'm* leaving on schedule," she said.

"Devon offered to let me stay with you until I found an apartment," Marcie said hurriedly to Michel. "I hope that's all right. I won't be here long. I'll try to find a place I can move into right away."

"There's no hurry," he said as they pulled up to the castle and the chauffeur came around to open the door. "You're welcome to stay as long as you like."

He turned to Shannon, but she was getting out of the car. She knew he felt obligated to extend the same invitation to her, and she didn't want to hear it so she quickly said good-night.

Shannon was too keyed up to be tired, but she needed some time alone to try and figure out her own personal dilemma. There had been so many ups and downs to the evening. She and Michel had run the gamut from barely speaking to easy camaraderie. That poignant moment by the fish pond had given her renewed hope. But then he became withdrawn again. By the end of the evening she no longer knew how Michel felt about her. And there wasn't much time left to find out.

Was his reserve due to the fact that he told her he couldn't have children? That would be a bitter pill for any man. Was he embarrassed that she knew?

Suddenly a blinding thought hit her! What if Michel was waiting to hear her say that it didn't matter? She had been so stunned at the time that her only reaction to the news was shock. But he didn't know that. His feeling of rejection would create just this kind of barrier between them.

It was a good thing he hadn't proposed convincingly that day. Michel would have been even more hurt if she hadn't been able to give him an answer. It took a lot of soul-searching before Shannon realized that she didn't have to give up her dream of having children. There were so many little ones waiting to be adopted into a loving home.

But there was only one Michel—the love of her life. Maybe it was wishful thinking on her part to believe they had a future together, yet if there was even the slimmest chance that he cared about her, she had to tell him how she felt.

With excitement churning in her veins, Shannon went out onto the terrace to see if Michel had come upstairs yet. Light was streaming from the windows of his apartment. She walked toward it, took a deep breath and knocked on the French door of the living room.

Michel had stripped off his shoes and shirt, then decided to look over a report he'd left in the living room. He wouldn't be able to sleep anyway.

It would be easier after Shannon left, he assured himself. He wouldn't have to go through the constant torture of appearing indifferent to her. In time he would forget how she felt in his arms, the yielding softness of her body, the delight on her beautiful face as he brought her joy.

Michel groaned. Who was he kidding? He would never forget her. She was the woman he'd been looking for all his life, the one he wanted to spend eternity with. And he couldn't even tell her he loved her.

When he heard the tap at his window, Michel froze. He realized it could only be Shannon on the terrace, and he didn't trust himself to talk to her right now. But it wasn't something he could avoid.

Shannon's heart plunged when she saw Michel's stern expression. Too late, she realized she should have waited until the next day. "I'm sorry I disturbed you. You're getting ready for bed."

After one quick glance at his bare chest, she looked away hurriedly. This was too reminiscent of that day at the lodge after Michel had finally pulled on his jeans. He'd looked exactly like this—chillingly remote.

She didn't know what a tight rein he was keeping on his emotions as he stared at her. The moon at her back had turned Shannon's hair into a spun-gold halo, and her eyes were dark blue pools in her shadowed face. He wanted to wrap his arms tightly around her and never let her go.

"I'll let you get to bed." She turned to leave.

But he opened the door wider. "No, it's all right. I was just going to look over some reports. Come in."

Shannon went inside reluctantly. Now that she was here, she didn't know how to begin. Especially since he'd made it clear that she was as welcome as rain at a picnic.

When she just gazed at him uncertainly, Michel said, "Did you want to tell me something?"

Only that I love you, she thought despairingly. *I hoped it would make a difference, but I can see now that it wouldn't.*

He was looking at her impatiently, so she said the only thing she could think of, "I just wanted to say that…um…it was a nice party after all, wasn't it?"

"You didn't come here to tell me that, Shannon. What's really on your mind?"

"All right," she sighed. "I'm here because this might be the last chance we'll have to talk privately. I'm going home on Sunday, as you know."

"I hope you enjoyed your stay here." He sounded as impersonal as a hotel manager.

"It was an experience I'll never forget." Shannon's cheeks flushed as she realized how that might sound. "I mean, I had a marvelous time. I can't begin to thank you for all your hospitality."

"It isn't necessary. I enjoyed having you." After a moment he said, "I suppose you're looking forward to getting home."

"Actually, I am. It will be nice to get back to normal. I guess I wasn't cut out for the life of a princess," she said with a slight laugh.

"It has its drawbacks like everything else."

Their conversation was so stilted and impersonal

that Shannon could have cried. She was tempted to say good-night and put them both out of their misery. Then her resolve stiffened. She had come for answers that she hadn't gotten yet.

Squaring her shoulders, she said abruptly, "I want to talk to you about that day at the lodge."

"Let it go, Shannon," he ordered.

"I can't. I was upset at the time, so I said some things I didn't mean, and maybe you did, too."

He ignored the questioning note in her voice. "Why are you bringing it up now? What good can it possibly do?"

"I'm afraid I was insensitive when you told me about your...um...your condition."

His jaw set grimly. "Is this your revenge? You want to gloat over my inadequacies as a man?"

"You're not inadequate! You must never think that."

"You mean I'm capable of performing the important functions," he said sardonically. "Yes, I know I can still give a woman pleasure. You demonstrated that."

Shannon's face paled at the way he'd demeaned that tender interlude, turning it into something cheap. But she dug her nails into her damp palms and continued doggedly, "I know the subject is painful for you. I only brought it up because I realize now that you might have misunderstood my response when you told me."

"What was there to misunderstand? As I remember, you greeted the news with a shocked silence," he drawled. "Then you advised me to see a specialist."

"Both of those reactions are normal," she protested. "You're in the prime of life. It's hard to believe there is anything you can't do."

"I'd rather not be reminded of it."

"I only wanted to tell you that it needn't be a handicap. You can still have a family. It doesn't matter whether you're a biological parent or not. The important thing is being a good father."

Michel looked at her impassively, but his emotions were churning under the surface. Was Shannon telling him it didn't matter to her, that she'd marry him in spite of his handicap? Hope flared through him, but he had to be very sure.

"You're talking about adoption," he said, forcing himself to sound disinterested. "What woman would settle for that when she could have her own babies?"

"If it was their only option, she would."

It wasn't the enthusiastic endorsement he'd been hoping for. Whenever he had fantasized this moment, Shannon had thrown her arms around his neck and told him she loved him, that he was the most important person in her life. Everything else could be worked out, as long as they had each other.

It was a nice fiction, but that's exactly what it was—a dream that was his alone. Shannon might think she believed what she had just said, but she would always know that *she* had had another option. He was deluding himself if he thought she wouldn't have regrets, wondering what her own babies would have been like. How could he rob her of the children she was entitled to have? He couldn't. Not if he really loved her. There would be a void in her life that nothing he had to give her could fill.

"I'm sure your advice is well meant," he said, gazing at her dispassionately. "But it isn't something I prefer to discuss."

"You were the one who told—"

"You're aware of the circumstances that led to my telling you," he cut in. "Which is another thing I don't want to talk about. It was a regrettable incident that never should have happened. I'm trying to forget about it, and I suggest you do the same."

If he had slapped her, Shannon couldn't have been more hurt. How could he refer to their enchanted interlude together as an "incident"? She hadn't expected it to mean as much to him, but didn't he feel anything? Besides regret that she'd caused him to violate his code of ethics. Shannon was grateful that at least she didn't get a chance to tell Michel that she loved him.

Lifting her chin, she said, "It seems we have nothing left to talk about. Don't worry, I'm sure your conscience will stop twinging as soon as I'm gone. Just remind yourself that the 'regrettable incident,'" she mimicked sarcastically, "wasn't that important to either of us." With her head held high, she marched to the French door and out onto the terrace.

If she had looked back, Shannon would have seen the desolation in Michel's eyes as he watched her walk out of his life.

The next day was Saturday, which meant Shannon had only one more day to get through. Who would have believed the trip she'd looked forward to so eagerly would end in such unhappiness?

Marcie came to her suite that morning for breakfast, which they had served outside on the terrace. Shannon only had juice and coffee, but her cousin requested a bowl of strawberries, followed by eggs benedict and a cup of café au lait.

"I don't know what Michel pays his chef, but the man could make a fortune by opening a restaurant," Marcie said as she poured cream on her strawberries. "Did you ever taste such divine food?"

"I don't know how you can eat like that and not gain weight," Shannon remarked.

"Good metabolism, plus an appreciation for any cooking other than my own." Marcie's grin faded as she gazed at her cousin. "It wouldn't hurt you to eat a little more. You're the only person I know of who lost weight on a vacation."

"You know what they say," Shannon said lightly. "You can never be too rich or too thin. I'll have to settle for thin."

"Seriously. You don't look like your old self. Do you feel okay? You have shadows under your eyes."

"That's because I don't have on any makeup yet. It takes a lot of time and concealer to get that natural look," Shannon said with a forced laugh.

"Don't try to sell me that. I've seen you straight out of the shower and you look great. Is it Michel? Did you two have another argument? It looked as if you were getting along all right at the barbecue."

"What can I do to convince you that I couldn't care less about Michel?"

"You could do a better job of hiding your feelings. When things are going smoothly, you light up like a birthday cake. The rest of the time you just go through the motions."

"You're imagining things. I'm a little tired, that's all. It's been a hectic two weeks and I'm running out of steam. I thought I could let my hair down with *you*."

"I hope that's all it is." Marcie was clearly skeptical. "But don't ask me to believe Michel didn't get to you."

"I'll agree that he's charming," Shannon said dismissively.

"You can do better than that. A man like Michel must have women trying to break down his bedroom door."

"Did you expect me to be one of them?"

"No, but you might have tried to loosen up a little. How is he supposed to know you're really interested in him if your relationship consists of a few chaste kisses? You *did* at least kiss him, didn't you?"

Shannon knew her expressive face had given her away once more. She could feel her pulse start to race when she remembered Michel's kisses not only teasing the corners of her mouth, but trailing a scorching, erotic path down her nude body.

Marcie was watching her intently. "That isn't all that happened, is it?"

Shannon forced herself not to react. "I'm sorry I told you about my lack of experience. It wasn't something I wanted to talk about then, and I still don't. All I will tell you is that it wouldn't have made any difference in our relationship if I had slept with Michel."

Marcie furrowed her brow as she tried to figure out if Shannon meant she had, or she hadn't. "Are you saying—?"

"Let it go, cousin." Shannon tried for a lighter note. "What do you and Devon have planned for my last day in paradise?"

Marcie looked as if she was about to say more, then thought better of it. "We decided to have a gala champagne dinner here at home, just the four of us. Because after that, a bunch of people want to stop by."

"That sounds very nice," Shannon commented.

If Marcie noticed her tepid tone, she didn't comment. "Devon wanted to plan something for today, too, but I told him I'd like to spend the day alone with you. I hope that's all right?"

"It's perfect! Let's have lunch and go shopping like we used to do at home."

"Sounds good. And if we have time, maybe you'll go with me to look at some apartments I marked in the newspaper."

"Okay, but I might cry. I'm going to miss you so much!"

"Me, too." As they clung together briefly, Marcie murmured, "Be happy, cuz. There are plenty of other fish in the sea."

Shannon wondered if Michel would show up for her farewell dinner. Her rush of pleasure when he appeared was tempered by the knowledge that his presence was almost obligatory.

Still it was a festive dinner—Devon and Marcie made sure of that. There were a lot of toasts, and the wine relaxed the tension between Shannon and Michel.

They didn't see much of each other during the rest

of the evening. So many people had come to say goodbye to Shannon that the evening flew by. When the guests started to leave, she was actually sorry the party was over.

Shannon had a dream about Michel, that last night in the castle. In the dream she had awakened to find him standing beside her bed. He was a faintly alarming figure in the darkness, tall and broad shouldered, with shadows masking his expression. Then the moon broke through the clouds and she saw the look of longing in his eyes.

When she opened her arms to him, Michel slipped into bed and took her in a close embrace. Somehow, they were both nude. She moved against him in ecstasy, greedy for the feel of his hair-roughened chest against her breasts, his rigid manhood at the juncture of her thighs.

Michel cried out hoarsely and wrapped his legs tightly around hers as his mouth possessed hers hungrily. His tongue explored the warm, wet recess while his hands aroused her with intimate caresses that fed her passion until it threatened to flame out of control.

When she whispered her urgent need, he parted her legs and plunged deeply, satisfyingly inside her. She arched her body into his and clung to him as his rapid thrusts intensified the pleasure almost unbearably. When the final burst of rapture thundered through their bodies, they both cried out their love.

In her wonderful dream, Shannon fell asleep in Michel's arms with a smile on her face.

She awoke feeling relaxed and happy, still under

the night's spell. Without opening her eyes, she turned on her side and reached out for Michel.

Like a balloon popping over a comic strip character's head, the dream self-destructed and reality returned. What a cruel joke her mind had played on her! Shannon had to force herself to get out of bed and face the day.

She was pale, but composed when she went downstairs sometime later, right before she had to leave. Goodbyes were always difficult, and this one would be especially painful, so she planned to keep it short. Her suitcases were packed and waiting for a servant to put them into the car that would take her to the airport.

Marcie and Devon were waiting for her, but Michel was nowhere in sight. Wasn't he even going to say goodbye? Shannon knew it would be easier that way, but it still hurt.

"I wish you'd let us drive you to the airport," Devon said.

"There's something to be said for not dragging out the farewells," Marcie remarked.

As Shannon looked at her gratefully, Michel came striding down the hall from his office. "I got an overseas call, and I had a devil of a time getting off the phone," he explained.

Shannon could only gaze at him wordlessly. His dark hair was ruffled as it had been in her dream. But then it was because she'd anchored her fingers in it while he'd possessed her completely. If only the dream wasn't still so achingly vivid, she thought despairingly.

A servant came downstairs with her bags, and the chauffeur carried them out to the waiting limousine.

"Well, I guess this is it," Marcie said, putting her arms around Shannon. "Call me when you get home. I want to hear everything that happened while we were gone."

Devon hugged her also. "Stay in touch with us, too," he said.

"I will," she promised. "I don't know how to thank you for making my visit so fantastic."

They both said all the polite things, which just happened to be true. Shannon felt she'd made a real friend.

The hardest part was saying goodbye to Michel. There were so many things she wanted to say, but some of them would be misconstrued, and it was too late for the others.

Finally she faced him and extended her hand. "I know it's inadequate, but thank you for everything."

He raised her hand to his lips and said, "Have a good life, my dear."

They gazed into each other's eyes for a long moment. Then Shannon went out the door and got into the waiting limo.

As the car drove away, she steeled herself not to look back.

Chapter Thirteen

Everybody wanted to hear about Bonaventure when Shannon returned to Los Angeles. She enjoyed describing the beautiful little country and telling how friendly the people were. What she didn't enjoy, was talking about Michel. Unfortunately, he was considered the main attraction.

Michel was irresistible to women. Even to women who had never met him!

Shannon immersed herself in work and tried to forget about Bonaventure and everything that had happened there. But even after the buzz died down at the office and with her friends, phone calls from Marcie were constant reminders, especially while she was still staying at the castle.

At first, Shannon wondered what Michel was doing and if he missed her. Those questions were answered after a couple of weeks. Michel was dating a succession of beautiful women, and he obviously didn't miss her. He was pictured at an endless procession of charity functions and theater openings, always looking heartbreakingly handsome, and a lot more carefree than he'd been when *she* was there.

Shannon could tell herself that his presence at the charity events was obligatory. But the candid shots in clubs and restaurants really hurt. The paparazzi always managed to catch his woman of the moment whispering in his ear, or click them dancing closer than necessary. The media were delighted. They commented on how much more social the ruling prince had become.

Marcie phoned one night, bubbling over with news that she'd gotten her first big order from a boutique in Cannes. "The samples I sent them sold out in a matter of days, and I have orders for so many more that I'm working nonstop."

"That's fantastic!" Shannon exclaimed. "You've accomplished a lot in such a short time."

"Actually, it's going on two months," Marcie said.

"Is it really?" Evidently time flew by even when you *weren't* having fun, Shannon thought wryly. In a way, Bonaventure was a distant memory, yet Michel's face was as clearly etched on her brain as if she'd seen him yesterday.

There was a click on the line and Devon said, "Are you through with girl talk? Can I join the conversation?"

"He's in Michel's office, and I'm in the den," Marcie explained.

Shannon was always glad to talk to Devon. He

asked about a very exclusive new club he'd heard of in L.A., and she teased him about knowing more about the local nightlife than she did.

Suddenly he said, "Hold on a second." Devon put his hand over the mouthpiece and said to his brother, who had just come into the office, "Somebody wants to talk to you."

Michel gave him a questioning look but took the phone. "Michel here. Who is this?"

He didn't have to give his name. That deep voice was as familiar as her own—and still had the power to stir her senses.

"Hello! Is anybody there?" he demanded, when she didn't answer immediately.

"You surprised me. I didn't know Devon was going to put you on. It's Shannon."

"Yes, I know. I remember your voice." And everything else about you, Michel added silently. "How are you?"

"I'm just fine," she said brightly. "I don't have to ask how *you* are. I seem to see your picture every time I open a magazine."

He made a sound like a low growl. "Damned paparazzi! They don't give you a minute's privacy."

"I guess that's what happens when you're a party animal," she said with a brittle little laugh.

"Are you glad to be back at work?" he asked, changing the subject.

"Oh, yes, very glad. I didn't realize how much I missed my job."

"Yes, work can be very satisfying. I keep trying to impress that on Devon."

She couldn't help smiling. "Just hang in there. You have to keep hoping."

"I tried that. It doesn't work," he said in a flat voice.

There didn't seem to be anything else to say. Before the silence became painful, Shannon said, "Well, I won't keep you. I know you're probably busy."

"That's all right." He paused for a moment. "Is there anything I can do for you?"

"No, but thank you for asking." Shannon thought she'd resigned herself to the fact that she'd never see Michel again. But hearing his voice brought back all the pain and longing. She couldn't take much more of this. "Well…it was nice talking to you."

"I'll get Marcie for you," he said somberly, gesturing to his brother. It was evident that Shannon was trying to get rid of him.

"Don't bother," she said. "We had already finished our conversation."

But a click told her that Marcie was back on the line. She'd hung up her extension when she heard Michel's voice. "Cuz? I thought of something else to tell you."

Shannon's misery suddenly boiled over. "Not now, Marcie!" she said sharply. "I have things to do."

Marcie was clearly shocked. "I'm sorry if I've been going on and on about my own affairs without giving you a chance to tell me what *you've* been doing. It's just that nothing this exciting has ever happened to me before."

Now Shannon felt even worse. "I'm the one who should apologize. I had to work late tonight for the third night in a row. I'm tired and cranky, but that's no excuse for snapping at you.''

''Hey, this is me, Marcie, you don't need an excuse. I wish you wouldn't work so hard, though. I suppose you're not eating, either.''

''I'm going to fix dinner as soon as you let me off the phone,'' Shannon promised.

It was true that she wasn't eating. Nothing appealed to her and she was tired all the time. She was languishing away like the heroine in an old Victorian novel, Shannon told herself mockingly. But she couldn't seem to pull herself together.

''Oh, Michel, what have you done to me?'' she whispered despairingly.

A couple of weeks later, when her fatigue persisted and she felt slightly queasy at times—like when a friend ordered a chili dog for lunch—Shannon knew she'd better see a doctor. She couldn't afford to get sick.

After giving her a thorough examination, the internist who was filling in for her vacationing doctor, said, ''From all the indications, you're a very healthy young woman. You shouldn't have any trouble.''

Shannon gave a sigh of relief. ''Do I need to take vitamins?''

''I suppose it wouldn't hurt, but you'd better ask your gynecologist first.''

''Why would I go to a gynecologist for something like that?''

''Because you're pregnant. I assumed that you knew.''

She stared at him in disbelief. "No! You're wrong. I couldn't be pregnant!"

He hesitated a moment before saying, "Birth control isn't one hundred percent foolproof."

"You must be wrong," Shannon insisted.

"Believe me, a first-year intern can diagnose a pregnancy. You're in the very early stages—about two months along, I'd guess. You can get another opinion—in fact, you *should* see a specialist—but I guarantee he'll tell you the same thing."

"I see," she murmured.

The doctor patted her hand. "Sometimes these things come as a surprise, but babies have a way of winning your heart."

Shannon wasn't listening. She felt slightly numb. Somehow she managed to answer coherently and leave the office.

She no longer doubted the doctor's diagnosis. Under different circumstances she might even have suspected it herself. But Michel couldn't have children! At least that's what he told her.

Pacing the length of her living room, Shannon felt angry and betrayed. Had Michel made up that story about being sterile, just in case something like this should happen? She'd always found his confession difficult to believe.

But the Michel she knew couldn't be that devious. She remembered his tenderness when they made love, his concern for her at all times. Michel might not love her, but he did care about her. When they'd talked on the phone that last time, hadn't he asked if she needed anything? It wasn't one of those polite offers that aren't meant to be accepted. He was really sincere.

That wasn't a man who would impregnate a woman and then simply walk away. He might even "do the honorable thing" if he knew. But what kind of marriage would they have if he felt trapped, even if she hadn't done it on purpose? No, Michel must never know. She would raise their baby alone, and it would never lack for love.

Shannon felt a rising excitement after she'd made her decision. Michel had given her something very precious, a part of himself that would be a bond between them forever.

From that day on, there was a marked change in her. Everyone noticed it. She was more relaxed, she started to eat sensibly and her sense of humor returned. She was also more beautiful than ever before. There was a kind of glow about her.

Michel, on the other hand, was going through hell. After Shannon left, he'd tried to distract himself with other women, one more beautiful than the next. It hadn't worked.

Shannon's face haunted him, awake or asleep. He imagined holding her in his arms, caressing her smooth skin, walking hand in hand with her. How could he live the rest of his life without her by his side?

He had picked up the telephone countless times to call her—and tell her what? I love you. Please marry me. I'll give you anything in the world you want—except children.

Michel became more miserable as their separation lengthened, not less so. Finally he came to a decision.

He had to stop agonizing over the situation and take a positive step.

No one could guarantee the success of a marriage, although admittedly theirs would be starting out under a handicap. All the reasons for not asking Shannon to marry him were still valid. But maybe their marriage would work out, against all odds. If there was even a glimmer of hope that she'd let him share her life, he had to find out.

Making a decision revitalized Michel. Devon noticed it immediately. "I'm glad to see you're feeling better," he remarked.

Michel gave him a startled look. Had his angst been apparent to everybody? It was a good thing he'd finally pulled himself together. "I'm fine," he answered briefly. "I'm glad you're here, Devon. I need to talk to you. I'm going away for a while and you'll have to take over for me."

"Isn't this rather sudden? You didn't mention any plans. Where are you going?"

"Something came up unexpectedly." Michel sidestepped the last question. "I doubt if you will run into any problems, but if one does arise, you can confer with the ministers. They've been briefed on all the current situations."

"How long will you be gone?"

"I'm not sure. Probably not long, but this will give you a chance to get a feel for the job."

Devon looked at his brother with concern. "There is something wrong with you, isn't there? Why won't you tell me what it is? I'm not some disinterested bystander. I want to be there for you!"

"I'm in perfect health, I assure you." Except for

one important flaw, Michel added silently. "I wish you'd stop worrying about me."

"I will if you'll let me come with you—wherever you're going."

"Somebody has to stay home and watch the store." Michel gazed fondly at his brother. Devon had the right stuff, as the Americans said. Bonaventure would be in good hands.

Shannon felt as good as she looked, physically at least. But she still had occasional bouts of melancholy. It was so sad that their baby would never get to know its father. Perhaps sometime in the future, after Michel was married, she could tell him about his child and the two could meet. Shannon knew in her heart that was only a fantasy.

When the sadness built and threatened her newfound serenity, she sometimes went shopping in the infants' department. The tiny little sweaters and bibs and such would put a smile on anyone's face.

But that Thursday night, nothing seemed to raise her spirits. She came home from work feeling depressed. If only Marcie were here. Everybody she loved was in Bonaventure.

Shannon was trying to watch television when the doorbell rang. It was probably her neighbor. She was a nice woman, but a non stop talker about nothing in particular. Shannon was tempted not to answer the door, but the television must be audible outside.

The smile she'd pinned on her face vanished when she opened the door and saw Michel. They stared at each other for what seemed like an eternity.

Then Shannon reached out and touched him. "Are you really here, or am I imagining this?"

"I'm here—to stay, if you'll let me."

He reached out and gathered her in his arms, holding her so tightly that she could feel his heart thundering. Or maybe it was her own. It didn't matter. She wasn't going to question a miracle!

They clung together, exchanging hungry kisses while their hands moved restlessly over the other's body, as if to assure themselves this was really happening.

When they finally paused for breath, Shannon said, "Why didn't you tell me you were coming?"

"I was afraid you'd tell me not to."

"How could I, when I missed you so much?"

"If I'd only known! I've been going through hell, thinking you didn't care."

"You didn't look miserable when you were with that succession of beautiful women." She closed the door and drew him inside and over to the couch.

"I was trying to forget you, but I should have known better." He scooped her onto his lap and kissed her lingeringly. "You make a lasting impression, my little love."

"How lasting, Michel?" Shannon looked at him searchingly. Why had he come? She was afraid to take anything for granted. They'd had too many misunderstandings.

"How about for the rest of our lives?" he said. "I want to marry you, if you'll have me."

Her fears vanished as she flung her arms around his neck and rained tiny kisses all over his face. "Of course I'll marry you! I'd given up hope that you were ever going to ask me.''

He captured her mouth and they kissed rapturously. But as their kisses became more torrid, Michel drew back slightly and his expression sobered. ''Are you sure that's what you want? I don't want to pressure you into anything.''

''Don't try to get out of it.'' Happiness bubbled through her like pink champagne. ''You asked me and I accepted. It's settled. We're getting married!''

''I'd be devastated if you changed your mind. I just wanted to remind you of my limitations. Think long and hard about what you're giving up, Shannon. I love you too much to take away your dream of having children of your own.''

''Darling Michel, *you* are my dream come true. You would be enough for me, even if we couldn't have children.''

It was the declaration he'd prayed for! He cupped her cheek gently in his palm, but his face was still serious. ''I know I could love an adopted child. I just want to be sure you could. It would break my heart if you had regrets.''

''There's nothing to be sorry about. We're the two luckiest people in the world.''

Before she could tell him about the baby, he said, ''I hope you'll still feel that way after I tell you I've decided to abdicate without waiting for Devon to marry. He's going to need help in making the transition. I owe it to him and the country to step aside so I can prepare him to assume responsibility. I just thought you should know.''

''Do you think I fell in love with you because of

your title?'' she demanded. "You don't really know me after all!''

"I know you're the sweetest, most wonderful woman in the world, and I love you with all my heart.'' He smoothed her long hair tenderly. "I never thought you were dazzled by my title. But you wouldn't be human if you didn't enjoy the perks that power bestows. I just wanted you to realize it won't be quite the same.''

"I couldn't care less. I told you I didn't want to be a princess.''

"I'm afraid you won't have any choice about that.'' He smiled. "I'll still be a prince, just not a ruling one.''

"If the only reason you're stepping down is because you can't have children, you might want to reconsider.''

"No, darling. Most of my subjects would reject an adopted child as successor to the throne. Some of the people would remain loyal to me, but that would be dangerously divisive. I couldn't do that to my country.''

"I'm not talking about adopted children. I'm pregnant, Michel,'' she said softly.

His reaction wasn't what she expected. At first he stared at her in bewilderment. Then as her astounding news sank in, his expression saddened.

"It's all right, darling. I can understand how it happened. I tried everything to forget you, too. But this doesn't have to change anything. I found out how joyless life can be without you, and I can't face the prospect. We'll raise your baby together. I just can't pretend it's my natural heir.''

Shannon had tears in her eyes. "You would give your name to another man's child?"

"It's your child, sweetheart. That's all that matters."

"Oh, Michel, you're too good to be true! When I think of what those doctors did to you, I'm just furious! Maybe your sperm count was low, but they shouldn't have told you that you could never father a child. They might at least have said it was unlikely."

He shrugged. "Because of my position, they had an obligation to tell me. What point would there have been in sugarcoating the pill? It's still just as bitter."

"Haven't you been listening to me? I'm telling you the doctors were wrong! That day at the lodge we conceived a baby together—*your* baby and mine. I've never been with another man."

He looked uncertain for the first time. "I'm not doubting you, but perhaps you're mistaken. Are you sure you're pregnant?"

She laughed joyfully. "You should have been here when I was all droopy and I couldn't bear the smell of food. The doctor says I'm about two months along, so you do the math. Two months ago I was in Bonaventure, and I'm sure you haven't forgotten that I was a virgin at the time."

It took a few minutes for Michel to absorb this miraculous turn of events. She watched his expression change as the proof of her astounding statement finally convinced him.

Then his face lit with incredulous joy. "I thought my life would be complete if only you'd marry me, and now you've made me even happier. What can I ever give you that would equal your gifts to me?''

''Your love is all I want,'' Shannon said as he took her in his arms. ''It's all I've ever wanted.''

EPILOGUE

The wedding of Shannon Lois Blanchard and Prince Michel Louis Danton de Mornay was covered by media from all over the world. It was the kind of romantic love match that appealed to people everywhere. A handsome prince finds his beautiful Cinderella.

They came in droves to line the streets for a glimpse of the limousines that brought the princess-to-be and her Prince Charming to the ancient stone church where they would take their sacred vows.

When Shannon got out of the car, the spectators were dazzled by her crystal-beaded satin gown with its long, flowing train. They had only a peek at her face beneath the white veil that billowed from a circlet of stephanotis and orange blossoms, but nothing could hide the happiness she radiated.

Every seat in the church was taken, and the buzz of excitement grew louder as someone stationed at the door said, "They're here!"

"I can't wait to see her gown," Mimi de Forest said. "She's going to make such a gorgeous bride."

"All of Michel's women have been gorgeous," her husband, Gerry, said. "But I'm glad he chose Shannon."

"No other woman had a chance after he met her." Judith Wainwright sighed happily. "Anybody could tell they were mad about each other. He was utterly miserable after Shannon went home, and we all knew why."

"It was his own fault for letting her go," Mimi said.

"You know how people in love are," Judith said indulgently. "I suppose they argued about something perfectly trivial, and then realized they couldn't live without each other. Oh, look, it's starting!"

First came the groomsmen, a stately procession of young men with solemn faces. Devon and Michel followed them, looking very tall and regal. There were a lot of whispered comments about how handsome they both were, especially Prince Michel. He would have been a rare prize even if he weren't a ruling monarch.

Next came Marcie in a pale blue dress, holding a large bouquet of white roses, blue iris and delphinium. Unlike the others, she didn't practice restraint. Her face wore a big smile as she nodded at friends sitting along the aisle.

But the bride was the one everybody was waiting to see. When she appeared in the entry a murmur ran through the crowd, a spontaneous tribute to the princess they were all prepared to love.

While others exclaimed over her exquisite gown and the lovely bouquet of white orchids and fragrant sprigs of lilies of the valley, Judith whispered, "I'm just sorry Shannon doesn't have any family here today, at least someone to walk her down the aisle."

"Everybody here is her family," Mimi answered with misty eyes.

Michel never took his eyes off Shannon as she made her slow progression to the altar. He held out his hand to her when she reached him, and the love in his eyes moved a lot of the women to tears.

The ceremony was impressive; everyone listened in rapt silence till the end. They stirred when Devon placed the ornate ceremonial crown on Michel's head. The priceless, bejeweled crown was only used for coronations and weddings, so everybody stared at it curiously. Beams of sunlight caught the huge central ruby and large surrounding diamonds, making them flash like streaks of fire.

The hushed silence was broken when Shannon lifted her veil and Michel placed a crown on her head. It was smaller and more delicate than his crown, a rosy shimmer of pink diamonds and pearls that sparkled and glowed with a warm intensity.

"That isn't the ceremonial crown," Judith exclaimed in a muted voice.

"It was his mother's favorite," Mimi said softly.

"But she didn't wear it at state functions, only for happy occasions like royal birthdays and such," Judith said.

"Can you think of a happier occasion?"

"It's a storybook wedding," Judith agreed. She stared intently at the bride and groom. "I wonder what they're saying to each other."

Michel was gazing into Shannon's eyes. "No princess will ever look as beautiful in this crown," he murmured.

"I just hope they will all be as happy as I am," she whispered with a radiant smile.

Their magical wedding would always be one of the two high points of Shannon's life—the other was the birth of their twins.

All parents think their babies are beautiful. But Prince Darcy Kenneth and Princess Drusilla Marie, were outstanding by any criteria. Both were rosy, healthy little cherubs with long eyelashes and infectious smiles. He had dark hair like his father's, and hers was light and tinged with red, instead of being the color of sunshine like her mother's.

Shannon joked about getting two babies for the price of one, but Michel said both were priceless, and she certainly couldn't argue with that. No babies were ever pampered more. Each had a nanny, and both parents spent a lot of time with their children.

As she looked at her own healthy, happy babies who had so much, Shannon vowed to devote her free time to helping needy children all over the world who had so little.

Michel was proud of her goal, but he let her know that he would support any decision she cared to make about her own personal time. He reminded Shannon of her dream of becoming a lawyer. "You don't have to postpone it any longer."

"Getting my degree would simply be an ego trip," she said. "I can do so much more good by being a public advocate for the needy—and incidentally, using your name to get people to contribute to the cause," she said, grinning.

"It's your name, too, darling." Michel took her in his arms and kissed her lingeringly. "I gave it to you, along with my heart and everything else I own."

"Your greatest gift was the family I've always wanted." She linked her arms around his neck. "And maybe in a year or so we'll add to it."

"I can't promise anything, but I'll certainly be happy to try," he said in a deep, smoky voice.

She smiled enchantingly as his arms tightened around her. "That's all any woman could ask for."

* * * * *

Silhouette®

SPECIAL EDITION™

is proud to present:

BABY TIMES THREE

an exciting new miniseries from popular author

VICTORIA PADE

Baby Times 3

HER BABY SECRET

SE #1503, on sale November 2002

Paris Hanley needed to get pregnant—fast!—
without letting wealthy Ethan Tarlington find out
her plan! But after she gave birth to a baby girl,
passions flared between the single mother and the
business mogul. What would Ethan do when
he discovered Paris's string of secrets?

**Don't miss the other two upcoming titles in
the BABY TIMES THREE series, on sale
January 2003 and March 2003,
from Silhouette Special Edition.**

Available at your favorite retail outlet.

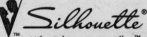

Silhouette®

Where love comes alive™

A powerful earthquake ravages Southern California...

Thousands are trapped beneath the rubble...

The men and women of Morgan Trayhern's team face their most heroic mission yet...

A brand-new series from
USA TODAY bestselling author

LINDSAY McKENNA

Don't miss these breathtaking stories of the triumph of love!

Look for one title per month from each Silhouette series:

August: THE HEART BENEATH
(Silhouette Special Edition #1486)

September: RIDE THE THUNDER
(Silhouette Desire #1459)

October: THE WILL TO LOVE
(Silhouette Romance #1618)

**November: PROTECTING
HIS OWN**
(Silhouette Intimate Moments #1185)

Available at your favorite retail outlet

Silhouette®
Where love comes alive™

 **Silhouette**®

COMING NEXT MONTH